Apache Fury

San Pueblo had never had a visitor quite like Zococa before. The bandit and his mute Apache companion, Tahoka, rode into the big city seeking nothing more than food and wine. But to their surprise they find thousands of other visitors filling the streets for the annual bullfighting festival.

In the meantime, a gang of skilled bank-robbers led by engineer John Harrison Weaver, arrive in the busy city carrying detailed plans that will enable them to break into one of Mexico's most secure banks. US Marshal Lucas McQuaid leads his posse over the border following the gang into San Pueblo and Zococa soon finds himself embroiled in a tangled web of death and horror.

With Tahoka at his side, Zococa has to face his most dangerous foe. But will they live to see the dawn?

Culture
& Sport

Apache Fury

ROY PATTERSON

A Black Horse Western

ROBERT HALE · LONDON

Typeset by
Derek Doyle & Associates, Liverpool.
Printed and bound in Great Britain by
Antony Rowe Limited, Wiltshire

Dedicated to Clint Walker

PROLOGUE

There were few men who had sought and found the dubious honour of being famous as a bandit on both sides of the long border which separated Mexico from the American states and territories. But one man had done exactly that and done it with flair.

Luis Santiago Rodrigo Vallencio was that man.

He had become known as the greatest of all the Mexican bandits who had ever lived and died plying their trade, yet his reputation was based mostly on his own exaggerations and ability to stretch the truth. Few of the deeds that he had been branded with had anything to do with him, but he joyously relished any and all additions to his long list of fictional accomplishments.

Even being wanted dead or alive on both sides of the border only made the handsome bandit feel more successful. To him life was just an adventure.

Boldly wearing his prized silver pistol on his left hip he continued to dare to be exactly what he knew the people wanted him to be.

He was their hero.

Riding always with the huge mute Apache brave known simply as Tahoka, the ever-smiling bandit remained as colourful as ever however many men dared to challenge him.

For Luis Santiago Rodrigo Vallencio continued to embellish his own reputation for the ears of those who listened to his tall tales.

Never once did he mention the acts of true valour and bravery which were the real part of his life. True heroism was not as interesting as the outrageous myths he invented.

Yet for all his fame, there was no one who knew his true identity.

To all who either loved or hated him, he was simply the left-handed one.

He was Zococa!

ONE

It was a cutting merciless wind that ripped along the long unmarked border. It had no respect for the noonday sun high above and totally obliterated its rays. The sandstorm whipped at everything in and around the small unnamed Mexican village of whitewashed adobes.

The two riders rode their horses around the side of the largest building until they found a place which the blinding sand seemed unable to reach. They dismounted and noticed several mules and two other saddle horses tethered to a long fencepole.

Zococa and Tahoka tied their mounts up at the side of the only building which remotely looked as if it might offer refuge and made their way inside.

The two bandits had been forced against their will to find a place where they could shelter their mounts until the storm subsided and it was possible to continue on towards their chosen goal.

The sand that covered both men disguised their identities until the young Mexican used his sombrero to beat it from their clothing. He stared across the room past the score of people at a wall against which stood two large wooden barrels. Countless years of dripping wine had stained the seasoned timber surfaces.

For a moment Zococa felt at ease and pointed at a wooden bench near the long bar. His tall power-fully built companion silently sat down and eyed the other people who milled around inside the cool building.

Zococa put his fingers into his shallow coat-pocket, and pulled out a few silver coins and dropped them on top of the warped plank that served as a counter.

'A jug of your sweetest wine, *señor*,' Zococa said to the nervous-looking man before pushing one of the coins forward on the damp plank. 'Do you have food?'

'No, *amigo*. Only wine,' came the nervous reply.

Zococa shrugged, and then picked up the remaining coins and slid them back into his pocket.

The keen instincts of the bandit knew that some-thing was not as it appeared in this small busy building. The face of the short man behind the counter had fear etched across it. It was not the fear of a man who was afraid of strangers but the fear of someone who knew that there was some-thing else brewing inside his small establishment. Something lethal.

Zococa turned his back to the assembled gathering and glanced down at the huge mute Apache warrior who was watching everyone closely. Zococa made a few secretive movements of his fingers to the knowing eyes of the Indian. Tahoka read the message and nodded.

Tahoka's face was like stone.

He knew that his younger friend was uneasy and so rested his own hand on top of his gun grip. With the keen eye of one who had often seen trouble exploding around his colourful friend, he remained alert.

Zococa turned back and faced the small man, who placed the jug of wine and two cloudy glass tumblers on top of the plank. He smiled at the man who seemed totally afraid.

'Thank you, *amigo*.' Zococa lifted the heavy vessel and poured himself a glass of the red liquid before leaning over and giving the jug to his friend.

Tahoka held it by its handle and drank from the neck of the jug as his eyes surveyed the room and the people who were standing in a large group in its centre.

The storm continued to rage outside and sand drifted in through the gap beneath the crude door. Zococa moved to the side of his seated partner but did not sit down. He leaned against the wall and sipped at the wine.

Nearly all of the men inside the room were dressed as most people in this region were. They wore simple white clothes that reflected the sun as they toiled beneath its cruel rays. Most of them, but not all.

Zococa lowered his left hand and tapped the shoulder of the drinking Indian. Tahoka read the fingers of the young bandit and nodded. Then Zococa slipped his hand back and released the safety loop from the hammer of his silver pistol with his thumb.

Tahoka stared through the crowd and saw what had alarmed Zococa.

The two bandits suddenly became aware that the faces of all the men dressed in white were as frightened as that of the small bartender.

Zococa moved one step to his right and stared through the throng of villagers at a pair of men seated in a darkened corner. These men were not Mexican, they were gringos and they were also well-armed. Too well-armed for simple cowboys.

The bandit took another sip of his wine and then placed the tumbler on top of the plank.

Over the years there had been many men like the pair in the corner to cross his and Tahoka's path. These men all looked the same. They had the blood of their victims still staining their unwashed clothing. They wore that blood like trophies. It reminded them of all the reward-money they had claimed.

Zococa knew without doubt that they were bounty hunters.

'I think that we should leave, my little rhinoceros.'

Tahoka placed the empty jug on to the bench beside him and rose to his feet. He stared over the heads of the fearful villagers inside the small room at the two unshaven men. His hands spoke to Zococa and the two men nodded silently to one another. Zococa adjusted his sombrero and tightened the cord knot under his chin.

'Let us go.'

Before they had taken a single step, the two heavily armed men stood up. The crowd scattered from between the bandits and the bloodstained gringos.

'Goin' someplace, boys?' one of the men asked as he cranked the mechanism of the Winchester in his hands.

Zococa stopped and faced the man. He studied both men with an eye trained to seek out any hint of weakness in those who dared to face him. Tahoka kept his hand on the grip of his holstered gun and began to move back towards Zococa.

The second bounty hunter waved a finger at the large Indian.

'A Mex with a stinking Injun. These must be the *hombres* that we've been looking for, Chad. This dude must be the one they call Zococa.'

The man with the Winchester smiled and displayed his rotten blackened teeth.

'Reckon so, Tom. There ain't no bounty on the redskin though. Seems hardly worth killing him as well.'

The bounty hunter called Tom waved a hand at

13

Tahoka as if shooing him away.

'It's your lucky day, Geronimo. Git going.'

Tahoka glanced across at the motionless Zococa.

'Meet me outside, little one,' Zococa said firmly.

The Apache warrior made frantic hand gestures to his partner but Zococa did not take his eyes off the bounty hunters in front of him.

'Ready our horses, *amigo*. The great Zococa can handle this alone.'

Reluctantly, the huge Apache obeyed the instructions of his friend. He pulled the door open and forced himself out into the sandstorm.

'How much did that wanted poster say this fancy Mexican is worth, Chad?' the second gunman asked.

'A few hundred as I recall,' came the reply.

Zococa smiled.

'It seems a very poor bargain, *señor.*'

'What does?'

'Risking death for a mere few hundred dollars,' Zococa replied.

The two men squared up to the confident bandit.

'They say you done killed twenty men,' the first bounty hunter said.

'I have killed two hundred men, *señor,*' Zococa lied.

The gathered crowd of villagers all made the same impressed noise together. Even facing possible death, the bandit could not help himself adding to his already inflated reputation.

'You ain't killed two hundred men,' the bounty hunter named Chad snapped.

'This number includes midgets, *amigo.*' Zococa flexed the fingers of his left hand as it hovered over the grip of his pistol.

'Midgets?' The first bounty hunter repeated the word.

'*Sí, amigo.* I count two midgets as being one grown man,' Zococa embellished.

The two men seemed confused as they took a step closer to their intended victim. They had never encountered anyone like Zococa before. They had seen their chosen victims smiling before but never so confidently.

'Dead or alive means dead in our books, Zococa,' the second man said as he rested his hands on the handles of his Colts.

'Do you wish me to wound or to kill you, *amigos*?' Zococa asked. 'The choice is yours.'

'Hush up and draw,' the first man screamed. He turned the barrel of his Winchester in Zococa's direction as his companion drew one of his Colts.

Before either of them had time to blink, Zococa drew his pistol and fanned its hammer twice. Neither bounty hunter had time to return fire. By the time the gunsmoke had cleared, Zococa had stripped them of their weapons and distributed them among the stunned but impressed villagers.

'Keep these guns, *amigos,* or, if you wish, sell them back to these men when I have gone.' Zococa grinned.

Zococa quickly removed the spent shells from his silver pistol and pushed new bullets into the smoking chambers before snapping it shut again.

He stared down at the two wounded men on the filthy floor and smiled. He had hit both men in their gun hands with an accuracy that amazed even himself.

'I could have killed you but I am the great Zococa. I show mercy to those who are less talented than myself.'

The bounty hunter named Chad stared up from the floor at the bandit as he nursed the hole in his gun hand.

'You're gonna wish you *had* killed us when we catch up with you, Zococa,' he threatened.

Zococa walked to the door and glanced over his shoulder.

'Do not follow Zococa. For if you do, I *will* surely kill you, *amigo.*'

Before either of the wounded bounty hunters could reply, the bandit had disappeared into the raging sandstorm. They listened to the two horses galloping away.

TWO

It sounded as all Mexican cities did after sundown. The music of guitars and trumpets echoed around its seasoned buildings as the residents celebrated the arrival of yet another night. Another opportunity to party the hours of darkness away.

The tall pinto stallion walked slowly through the thriving streets of San Pueblo with the black gelding trailing its every stride. Zococa teased his reins and glanced over his shoulder at the massive Apache brave who followed. They had not entered such a large Mexican city for several years and had forgotten just how active they became once the blazing sun had set.

Normally the bandits would use the less illuminated streets when they entered smaller towns on either side of the long, seemingly endless border which separated the two vastly differing cultures. But there were so many people roaming around San Pueblo that two more ought to have gone unnoticed.

They would have, had one of them not been

17

riding the handsome pinto stallion. Yet this was one night when few of the citizens gave either rider a second look because they were all in a hurry to reach their destination.

Zococa drew his silver-embossed black reins to his chest and stopped the powerful horse. He was staring open-mouthed at a sight that stirred the blood in his veins. Even from a quarter of a mile away, the massive edifice resounded with the cheers of the patrons who had already entered it.

Tahoka drew alongside the pinto and looked at his friend's face before turning his attention to the curved walls of the huge bull-ring.

'Is it not wonderful, my little rhinoceros?' Zococa asked his silent friend.

The mute Apache gestured with his fingers and hands in reply but the younger rider did not see anything but the circular structure bathed in torch-light. Zococa had never seen anything that lured his flamboyant nature as much as this. There must have been a hundred flags of differing sizes and colours blowing in the gentle evening breeze as they hung from the walls of the bull-ring above the dozens of entrances.

'I have heard many stories of these places, *amigo*. I want to go in and savour the atmosphere.' Zococa breathed heavily as his heart raced.

Tahoka tapped his friend's arm just hard enough to get his attention. Zococa looked at the gigantic Indian who was pointing to his mouth and then his belly.

'Why are you always hungry, Tahoka? Have you no romance in your heart? Look at the magnificent bull-ring. That is where men are men and they prove it every day of their lives.'

Tahoka spoke again with his hands.

Zococa's lower lip seemed to move over his thin moustache as he pondered the question.

'What do you mean by asking me what these men do? Is it not obvious? Look at the pretty pictures. They fight the bull. It is, I am told, most wonderful.'

Tahoka moved his hands to either side of his braided hair and snorted.

Zococa patted the shoulder of his friend. 'Exactly, my little one. They fight the bulls.'

The Apache brave shook his head and rubbed his stomach once again. He was very hungry.

'Without these men fighting the bulls, there would be no meat to put in your fat belly.'

Tahoka looked around them and spotted a small cantina which seemed to be doing a good trade in selling food to the people who were heading steadily towards the large bull-ring.

Zococa watched as the mute Apache tapped his feet into the sides of his gelding and aimed the horse toward the aromatic cantina.

'Where are you going? I thought we would go and see the bull being fought by the brave ones,' called Zococa.

He watched as his friend slid from his saddle and tied the black mount to a hitching rail outside

19

the cantina. Tahoka curled his finger at the younger man. Zococa pulled the head of his horse to the right and tapped his spurs into its flanks. The stallion responded instantly and brought the bandit to the side of the waiting Tahoka.

'I know that you are most hungry, *amigo*.' Zococa dismounted and looped his reins around the rail.

Both men entered the comparatively peaceful cantina and inhaled the aroma of the food which was being constantly prepared by four cooks. Zococa removed his sombrero and followed the taller man to a quiet corner where a round table awaited them. As on all the tables within the cool whitewashed building a candle burned in the neck of an old wine-bottle.

'We shall eat and then go and see the bulls being fought.'

Tahoka asked him another question.

'I do not know how they fight the bulls. They probably have very big guns.' Zococa sighed, tossing his sombrero on to an empty chair.

Zococa produced two long thin cigars from the silver case he wore over his heart, picked up the bottle and used the candle to light Tahoka's cigar and then his own. After replacing the bottle he snuffed out its flame with his thumb and index finger.

Zococa did not like sitting so close to a light. He had found that it drew moths and sometimes the bullets of those who dared to collect the reward money on his head.

'This is very boring,' he announced to his impassive friend. 'We could be in the big building where they kill the bulls. We could be having much fun.'

Tahoka inhaled on the cigar and then spoke with his fingers again.

'What do you mean by saying that you would rather wait here for them to bring the dead bulls to us?'

The Indian pointed to his mouth and pretended to chew.

'You have no class, my little elephant.'

Zococa turned and watched the four female cooks selling their wares through the large open window to the hundreds of passing people. Three of them were well-rounded but the fourth was still young enough to be shapely.

'That one is very lovely.' Zococa raised his eyebrows and touched his thin black moustache with his little finger. 'I think she will be begging me to make love to her very soon.'

Tahoka raised his hands as if about to say something. Zococa waved a finger at the frowning man.

'Do not keep chattering. You are starting to give me the headache, *amigo*. If she throws herself at me, what can I do? Insult her?'

To the disappointment of the bandit and the amusement of the huge Apache brave, it was not the youngest cook who turned and walked over to take their orders, but one of the larger females.

Zococa's smile greeted the handsome woman.

'You would like wine with your food, *señor*?' she

asked the bandit, fluttering her long eyelashes.

'*Sí*, my beautiful one. Two bottles of your best wine.' The words tripped from Zococa's mouth. He sucked the end of his cigar and watched the woman blushing.

'What do you wish to eat, my bold one?' She moved closer to where Zococa was sitting and did not stop until her hips were touching his arm. 'Chilli and tacos? We have steak cooked in the finest brandy, and beans. Many, many beans.'

Tahoka nodded frantically but she did not notice the hungry Indian. She only had eyes for his handsome friend.

Her hand was teasing the black hair of the seated Zococa as she pushed her large bosoms into the side of his face.

'That sounds splendid. We will have two orders of all of that, *señora*.' Zococa felt sweat trickling down the side of his face as he sensed one of her nipples beneath the white blouse touching his ear.

Her finger touched the chin of the bandit.

'I am not married, you lucky man.'

Zococa placed the cigar between his perfect teeth and watched as she returned to her colleagues and started preparing their order. She was now singing and looking over her shoulder as her ample rear rocked back and forth.

Tahoka snapped his fingers and got Zococa's attention. He spoke with his hands to the younger man who was trying to smoothe his hair down again.

'You are right, little one. She is very friendly, I think.'

THREE

It was probably the largest bank south of the border. If there was one bigger, nobody had ever heard of it. San Pueblo required such a mammoth edifice because nearly half the region's taxes were stored deep in its vaults, in addition to the federal budget for the entire Mexican army.

On any given day an eighth of Mexico's total wealth was housed deep in the secured chambers of the government-owned San Pueblo bank. The vault itself stretched over 200 feet in width and was of an equal length. The cast-iron body of its safe stood twenty feet in height and was reputed to have taken three years to complete.

The whole metal complex had been riveted together in ten-feet-wide sections inside the bank's foundations before the rest of the building had been constructed over it. Even though the bank itself was impressive above ground, what lay hidden beneath was beyond most people's wildest imaginings.

Fifty guards protected the bank at all times,

working in three eight-hour shifts. It was probably the best protected structure outside the emperor's palace in Mexico City. But only the powerful citizens of San Pueblo had good reason to want to protect this monument to greed. For it contained so much gold and silver that even the most fanciful of thieves could never have come close to guessing exactly how much wealth was buried deep in its apparently impenetrable vaults.

A wealth that had been harvested from the poorest of souls in one unfair tax after another.

San Pueblo had been nothing more than just another town before the government decided that it was exactly the right place to build their financial fortress. It had soon become a city when it lured thousands of people into its spider's web.

People had been drawn there in the hope of bettering their lot, and then found themselves trapped in a situation from which escape was almost impossible.

The rest of San Pueblo had grown quickly around the bank and the army fortress which stood less than a hundred yards behind it. Within a generation a sleepy peaceful town had become a city that taxed everything except the air itself and fed off the backs of its inhabitants like a parasite.

During the height of the bullfighting season the city played host to thousands of visitors. Stealthily those in power drained those visitors of cash by imposing taxes upon everything that people use to lead a civilized existence.

For all its bright lights and temptations, San Pueblo was a city designed to strip the flesh from the ignorant masses and make them be grateful for the privilege.

The city streets were indeed swollen by those who had nothing more on their minds but to enjoy the bullfighting season but there were those who had come to San Pueblo willingly to attempt the impossible.

Their ambitions were far grander and hinged on the fact that they were willing to risk their lives by attempting to rob the bank that lay at the very heart of the city itself.

The seven Delaware riders who had arrived before sunset were confident that they could rob the bank and escape with a million dollars' worth of gold bullion before anyone in San Pueblo was any the wiser.

For most men this would have been just a wild ambition, but not for the men from Delaware.

These were no ordinary bank robbers.

They were the best at what they did and what they did was rob banks. But unlike most men who entered this almost suicidal profession simply because they were capable of using a gun and had a fast horse, these seven men were skilled engineers.

For ten years they had worked exclusively for Uncle Sam and had designed and constructed everything from bridges to bank vaults. They had learned not only how to design and build these things but how to dismantle them as well.

What could be put together could be taken apart.

That had been the key to their success. For these men did not blindly enter a bank with their guns blazing in the hope that they would fare better than the Younger brothers and manage to escape unscathed. These men used the science of their profession to work out in the smallest of details how to accomplish the impossible.

There was nothing that was beyond these men.

John Harrison Weaver had led his team to and from nearby Tamaulipas. They had not been there to rob anyone but to do the vital research at the local government buildings. For in Tamaulipas every detailed plan of every Mexican bank was recorded.

Tamaulipas held the answers to all their questions.

The seven men had spent ten days copying every detail of the San Pueblo bank's vault plans. Then they had studied the crude underground sewer system which lay beneath the better part of San Pueblo. Another week was spent working out how such a bank vault could be taken to bits and how they could escape without detection.

Added to this, maps of the local terrain had given John Weaver and his team the vital knowledge they required to know exactly how to disappear without trace.

John Weaver and his associates were no mere

bunch of bank robbers, they were engineering experts. Soon they would bring that expertise to bear on the bank which, it was said, was impossible to rob.

It was a challenge, but one that these men were capable of meeting head on.

One they found totally irresistible.

FOUR

Zococa staggered down the tiled staircase and then sat down next to Tahoka. The large singing cook seemed to float from step to step as she followed him to the cantina.

'You are indeed the great Zococa,' she whispered into his ear. She pinched his cheek and then danced back to her three friends and resumed her chores.

For the first time since the two men had entered the cantina, they noticed the four women chattering. Every so often, one of the women would look over her shoulder and either wink or wave at the exhausted bandit.

Tahoka was still eating. He had continued even after the well-endowed female cook had dragged Zococa up to her bedroom. He chewed and watched as Zococa managed to pull a cigar from his silver case and place it between his teeth.

The Apache brave was never one to show any emotion but there was the hint of a smile on his face.

'Say nothing, my little one,' Zococa said, striking a match and touching the tip of the cigar. He barely had enough energy left to suck in the smoke but needed something to restore his strength. 'She was most insistent. I tried to resist but she was so strong.'

Tahoka picked up his wine-bottle and finished what was left inside its black glass.

'I have never met such a strong woman, *amigo.*' Zococa shuddered as he recalled everything that had occurred during the previous thirty minutes.

Tahoka's hand touched the sleeve of the younger man and then pointed in the direction of the open doorway. Somehow Zococa managed to turn his head and stare through the smoke which drifted up from his cigar.

The sight that greeted his tired eyes made him sit upright.

'What are they, my little one?'

Both bandits watched as three men dressed in the most elaborate of costumes entered and made their way to the next table. Zococa blinked hard and then realized that his eyes were not deceiving him. He was actually seeing the vision that had caused Tahoka to stop eating, even if only momentarily. The first man wore blue, the second red and the third pink. Their tailored costumes were covered in pearls and other decorations. They had their hair greased and tied into neat pony-tails. These men were indeed different.

Who were they?

The three men were clad in the most colourful outfits that either Zococa or Tahoka had ever seen. They were not matadors because they had seen the posters of matadors in the town square.

Yet they were dressed so outrageously that Zococa knew that they had to have something to do with the bullfights. He was intrigued.

'Who do you think they are?' Zococa asked his friend.

Tahoka lifted the last scrap of food off his plate and pushed it into his mouth. He then wiped his fingers on his buckskin shirt-front and leaned back in his chair. He could not care less what these men were.

Zococa stared at the bullwhips that were coiled and hanging from the men's hips. He noticed that the three men had noted his interest in them and were smiling in his direction.

'Do you men work in the bull-ring?'

All three roared with laughter at the naïve question. The man in pink leaned forward in his chair towards the bandit.

'*Sí, amigo*. We are the men who control the bulls and make them go into the ring to fight.'

Zococa's eyebrows rose.

'Where are your guns?'

The man pulled his whip loose and uncoiled it on the floor of the cantina.

'This is all we need.'

'A whip?' Zococa stared at the woven leather which was all of fifteen feet in length. He frowned.

'But what can you do with a mere whip, *señor?*'

The man in the pink costume rose to his feet, held the grip of the whip in his hand and looked around the empty tables within the cantina. All of them had a candle burning in the neck of a bottle.

The man raised his wrist a few inches and then flicked the whip gently. The tip of the whip snuffed out one of the candle-flames. The man then turned and extinguished another candle-flame with his long whip.

Within the space of sixty seconds the man had used his bullwhip to put out every single one of the candles. He then sat down and stared at the bandit who was in awe of the unexpected feat.

'Amazing!' Zococa exclaimed.

'Would you like to buy this whip from me, *señor?*' the man asked.

Zococa stood up with a broad smile on his face.

'*Sí, amigo.*'

Tahoka slowly shook his head as he watched Zococa haggling with the man dressed in pink. If there was one thing the young bandit could not resist, it was a new toy. By the time the massive Indian and the handsome bandit were leaving the cantina, Zococa had the whip hanging over his hand-tooled holster.

'Did you see what you can do with one of these, my little rhinoceros?' Zococa marvelled as he gathered up his reins and stepped into his stirrup.

Tahoka shrugged and made a few simple hand-gestures in reply. As Zococa sat on his saddle he frowned.

'I know it was the man and not the whip that flicked the flames from those candles. I am not a fool.'

The Apache nodded and turned his mount to face the street.

'Zococa.' The voice of the cook rang out through the large window of the cantina. 'Do you and your *amigo* want to stay here for the night? It is very late . . .'

Zococa looked down at the smiling face of the rotund cook who obviously wanted more from the bandit than he was either willing or able to give. The three smiling faces of the other females made him even more nervous.

'I think this place is most dangerous. We must find a safer place to stay tonight, Tahoka.' Zococa spurred his pinto stallion and rode along the still-noisy streets of San Pueblo.

The Apache brave pointed at the huge arena which was still filled with the sounds of thousands of cheering people. He asked if his friend still wanted to see a bullfight.

Zococa shook his head as his horse cantered. 'Not tonight. This night I am strangely tired.'

FIVE

Lucas McQuaid had a reputation. It was well-founded. The fifty-two-year-old lawman had ridden south of the border for only one reason and that was to dispatch his own brand of justice. Yet he was no mere bounty hunter, he was one of that rare breed of US marshals who actually knew his business.

For whereas most men who pin stars on their chests do so simply because they have grown weary of drifting, Lucas McQuaid was a different kettle of fish. It was not vengeance or boredom that drove him in pursuit of the lawbreakers, but an appetite for solving puzzles.

He had had many varying careers during his eventful life, most of which had honed his brain until it was so sharp, he could actually out-think the men he chased. Some had said that he had second sight but McQuaid himself simply considered it as nothing more than logical thought.

Although a marksman with both handgun and carbine, McQuaid had never been one to simply

37

dispatch the men he had hunted with his Winchester or the deadly pair of Remingtons that hung from the two crossed gun belts that straddled his girth. That would have been too easy.

His was a more tried and trusted method.

Lucas McQuaid used his great intellect to outwit his prey. He had suffered few failures in the last two decades during which he had plied his trade.

It was said that once McQuaid was on your trail, you were doomed. He applied his trained mind to anticipate where those he was tracking would go. To be one step ahead of them. To know what they were thinking even before they did. There had even been occasions when McQuaid had been so accurate in his deductions that he had actually been waiting in towns for those he was chasing to arrive.

Marshal McQuaid was indeed no ordinary lawman. But then he had received an excellent training in the career of which he had become a master. A few years with the famed Texas Rangers had only added to his knowledge of the terrain south of the Rio Grande. Now back in the saddle with the US marshal's badge on his vest, McQuaid had ridden into Mexico looking for answers to the questions that those whom he was chasing had posed.

How could it be that three of the most impenetrable banks in Texas had been robbed without anyone even knowing that anything was happening until it was too late?

McQuaid had already worked out who could have executed those robberies. From the outset it was obvious to the large lawman that this was no ordinary bank robber and his gang. These jobs had been planned with such attention to detail that it cast a light in a totally different direction.

These robberies had been the work of men who knew what they were doing and followed the instructions of their leader to the letter.

Lucas McQuaid had defied his many advisers and started to look for men who had worked either in or around the trio of banks. The name of one man had screamed at the marshal out of the mountains of paperwork. The name of a certain John Harrison Weaver. The papers did not call him a bank robber, it stated that he was a civil engineer.

McQuaid liked that. It seemed that he was in hot pursuit of a professional man. A man who had had an education such as himself. This was going to be an intellectual duel. A battle of wits to find who was the smarter of the pair. The fox or the hound. There were six other names that also matched the three banks in question but each of those were of men who worked in the construction team headed by Weaver.

McQuaid had been like a dog with a bone. Whatever else anyone might say, he knew that he was on the right track. He knew that John Weaver was his man.

Nothing could dissuade him from his chosen course. He formed a ten-man posse and then, gaining government permission to try to hunt down the seemingly innocent seven men over the border in Mexico, headed off on their trail.

Weaver was clever though and left little for the lawman to trail. Yet even crumbs were enough for McQuaid. He managed to lead his posse after the man and his team with a single-minded resolve that few could match.

With every mile, McQuaid had grown to admire Weaver even more than he had when studying the three Texan robberies. There was never any violence and everything was done to almost military precision. If Weaver was his man, McQuaid knew he might have finally met his equal.

It had been a long tedious journey, which had covered more than 200 miles, but at last the wily lawman knew exactly where Weaver and his crew were headed. Everything pointed to one place. San Pueblo.

And in the Mexican city there was only one possible target that could lure such men.

The sun was rising as McQuaid led the ten riders into the outskirts of San Pueblo.

SIX

The boisterous roosters who awoke Zococa and Tahoka were living dangerously. If they had been within range of the silver pistol holstered in the gun belt, they would surely have died of lead poisoning. The Mexican bandit rolled over in the straw and stared around the hayloft of the two-storey barn.

'I have died and ended up in a pile of straw?' Zococa questioned, brushing his clothing down.

The two men had consumed a lot more wine after leaving the cantina than either of them could remember. Exactly how they had ended up in the high loft above so many aromatic horses, including their own, was still a blurred mystery.

Zococa crawled to the open loft door and shielded his eyes against the morning sun before realizing where they had spent the night.

'Are you awake, little one?' Zococa asked the snoring Indian.

Zococa rubbed his temples vigorously and tried to stop the veins throbbing so noisily, but the numbness remained inside his head.

'I am awake, I think.' Zococa looked at his slumbering confederate and then managed to rise to his feet. 'I think I do not remember how we managed to arrive here.'

Tahoka's eyes opened suddenly when he felt his bare feet being kicked. The Apache brave rolled over and looked up at Zococa with a pained expression on his face.

'How did we get here?' Zococa asked again.

Tahoka sat upright and shook his head. Straw fell over his lap from his long hair. He closed one eye and tried to focus with the other on his friend. Tahoka made a few gestures with his hands and watched as the bandit nodded.

'You are right, *amigo*. We could not find anywhere to stay and then paid the stableman to allow us to sleep up here.' Zococa felt no satisfaction from recalling the details of their drunken night. He sniffed the air and then looked down at the horses below them. 'I must have been very, very drunk.'

Tahoka agreed.

Zococa made his way back to the open hayloft door again and studied the view. The bull-ring did not seem so interesting in the cold light of day. All its excitement had evaporated. Then he noticed the large sandstone buildings which dominated the skyline, and wondered what they were. Unlike others who had arrived in San Pueblo the previous day, he did not recognize the bank nor the army fortress behind it.

'What are those big buildings, Tahoka?'

The Indian crawled to his friend's feet and squinted out to where Zococa was pointing.

He made a few suggestions with his hands and the handsome bandit began to smile.

'Very good, little one. I like your imaginative ideas. I agree with you that they could be the homes of rich people but I am not so sure about them being brothels.'

Tahoka shrugged.

'If they are, business must be very good here.' Zococa inhaled the morning air and then coughed. He had not risen so early for a very long time. The roosters were to blame.

Tahoka slipped on his moccasins and then clambered upright. His head was filled with the fog that only a lot of very good wine can create inside a man's skull. He picked up his gun belt and strapped it around his middle. With a few carefully aimed movements of his fingers, he spoke to the bandit once more. Zococa plucked his own gun belt from where it had hung for hours, then put it around this hips and buckled it up.

'We still have many dollars left from our last little adventure, *amigo*. We do not have to look for any business for many weeks, I think.'

Tahoka nodded and looked at the saddle-bags that lay beside the coiled bullwhip. He then remembered more of the previous evening than he cared for.

Zococa's eyes lit up as he saw the whip.

'My whip !' he exclaimed joyfully.

Tahoka shook his head and pointed to the small red mark on the back of one of his hands. It looked as raw and painful as it actually was.

'How did you hurt yourself, Tahoka?'

The Indian inhaled until he was at his full height and then explained how, the night before, Zococa had tried to use the black-braided leather weapon to show how easy it was to snuff out a candle-flame with the fifteen-foot-long whip.

'I did it?' Zococa asked innocently.

Tahoka nodded frantically and used his hands to try and let his partner know exactly how bad he was with it.

'You are saying that I hit you and I was aiming at a candle, *amigo?*' Zococa raised both eyebrows and wondered why he still could not recall the incident. 'You should not have been standing so close to the candle. This is a dangerous weapon in the wrong hands.'

Tahoka snorted and told the younger man that he had been standing behind Zococa at the time.

Zococa grinned sheepishly. 'But that was when I was drunk. Now I am sober, you will see what an extra string to my bow this will be for the great Zococa.'

Tahoka shuddered when he watched Zococa picking up the coiled bullwhip and running the palm of his hand over its shining surface.

'I think I ought to practise.'

The Apache warrior continued shaking his head.

'Be brave, my little rhinoceros,' Zococa said as he uncoiled the long whip and started to test its weight in his hand.

Nervously, Tahoka moved to the other end of the loft and pointed at the loft door.

Zococa knew exactly what his companion meant. He placed the saddle-bags in the sunlight and then took a half-dozen steps backwards. He raised the whip in his left hand. The smiling bandit was filled with confidence as he looked over his shoulder at the brooding Apache.

'Do not fret, little one. This time you shall see that the great Zococa was made to use the whip.' The bandit swung the whip around his head and then brought his arm down quickly. The whip was no longer in the palm of his hand but wrapped around a wooden support beam above his head.

Tahoka watched silently as his embarrassed partner reached up, untangled the bullwhip from around the beam and then started to take aim once again.

'This time I will hit it.' Zococa cracked the whip.

He felt the end of the long whip catching something behind him. It was Tahoka. Slowly the handsome face of Zococa turned and looked over his shoulder at the massive Indian who was holding his right shin.

'Why do you insist on getting in the way, little one?'

Tahoka's eyes narrowed. He knew that there was no safe haven in the high barn loft whilst Zococa held the bullwhip in his hand. He began to clamber down to where their horses were stabled next to the dozens of other mounts. As he reached the floor he heard the whip cracking again and this time Zococa's voice calling out in pain.

There was almost the hint of a smile on his face as he sat down next to his black gelding.

Suddenly the smile evaporated when the giant Indian noticed the sun glinting off the stars on the chests of the eleven riders who were pulling their mounts to a halt outside the open barn doors. Tahoka could hear the sound of his companion complaining about his black whip in the loft above his hiding-place in the shadow of the horse-stalls.

The Apache moved silently, using the cover of the horses and their stalls to shield himself from any prying eyes that might have spotted him. Tahoka crawled beneath the belly of the pinto stallion towards the ladder.

He had to try to silence Zococa before the gringo lawmen heard him and investigated.

Marshal Lucas McQuaid dismounted first outside the barn and then nodded to the ten members of his posse. They all carefully got down from their horses and dusted themselves off. It had been a long ride that none of them, except McQuaid himself, had expected when they set out.

The marshal stared around the quiet streets and the colourful litter that remained as a reminder of the previous night's festivities. McQuaid knew his work was not going to be plain sailing when he saw the posters pasted to practically every wall within view. There were more than enough people living in San Pueblo without the additional visitors who flooded here to enjoy the bullfights, he thought.

'Where the hell is the livery man?' one of the deputies asked McQuaid, angrily rubbing his numb rear. 'I need me a long bath and an even longer beer.'

'This is Mexico, Ralph. They don't watch the clocks the same way as us,' the marshal observed. 'He'll be along pretty soon, I reckon; as soon as he smells the dollars in our pockets. Then we can make our way to the bank and take us a look.'

Tahoka secretly climbed back up the fixed wooden ladder at a speed that amazed even himself. Without a moment's hesitation he caught the end of the whip in full flight with his hands and then raised his fingers to his lips and indicated to Zococa that they might just be in a lot of trouble.

Zococa edged cautiously back to the loft door. Silently he dropped on to one knee and listened to the men talking below them. Tahoka pointed to his own chest and traced out the shape of a star.

'Lawmen?' Zococa whispered curiously. 'Do you think that we have been followed all the way from Texas?'

Tahoka nodded and began rolling the whip back into a coil as he watched his friend straining to hear what the men were saying.

'So you reckon that this gang will try and rob the bank here, marshal?' the voice of one of the posse asked.

'If my figurin' is right, I sure do,' McQuaid replied.

'I hate bank robbers,' Ralph Lee snarled. 'They're nothing but vermin.'

In the loft high above them Zococa's eyebrows had risen up his throbbing brow as the words 'bank' and 'robbers' raced through his brain. He tried to get a peek at the men milling around beneath their vantage point but knew it was far too risky even to try. He had to be content with just listening.

'How we gonna handle this, Marshal?' a deputy named Charlie Black asked.

McQuaid rubbed his jaw. 'Not the way you're thinking, Charlie.'

'What ya mean?' another of the posse piped up.

Lucas McQuaid sighed heavily and found his charged pipe in his vest pocket. He pushed the tobacco down into the bowl and then gripped the stem in his teeth.

'The varmint I'm after ain't no Jesse James. He's a man who has brains enough to know how these bank vaults are built. He and his men don't go round shooting towns up, they sneak in and out like phantoms.'

Ralph Lee frowned. 'I don't get it.'

'You mean they can get into a bank without anyone noticing, Lucas?' Charlie Black asked. 'How?'

'If we can figure that, we'll catch them red-handed.' McQuaid struck a match and puffed on the stem of his pipe until he disappeared in a cloud of smoke. 'Where in tarnation is that stable-man?'

Zococa's eyes brightened. He was intrigued. The bandit removed his jacket hurriedly and grabbed hold of a moth-eaten poncho that was hanging from a rusty nail near the open loft doorway. He pulled it over his head. He removed his gun belt and handed it to his friend. Then he picked up some hay, rubbed it into his hair and moved to the ladder.

Tahoka stood open-mouthed as he watched Zococa starting to descend the broad wooden steps.

49

'This shall be amusing, my little elephant.' Zococa rushed down into the dark barn and then walked with a fake limp to the large doorway where the posse were gathered.

'Hello, *amigos*,' Zococa said in his worst impression of an old man as he stooped and stared up at the lawmen.

Lucas McQuaid pulled the pipe from his mouth and stared in disbelief at Zococa, who was rubbing the nose of the marshal's horse.

'Is this your barn, mister?' McQuaid asked.

'*No comprendo, señor.*' Zococa limped around the men cooing at their mounts.

'They got some real geniuses around here, Marshal,' Lee commented as the deputies circled McQuaid.

McQuaid pulled out a few silver dollars from his pants pocket and handed them to Zococa. He then indicated to the horses.

'Look after our horses. Do you understand?'

Zococa made a face. 'Horses. *Sí, señor.*'

'What's the name of the leader of the gang, Marshal?' Black asked McQuaid.

'Weaver. John Harrison Weaver, Charlie.' McQuaid led the men down in the direction of the large sand-coloured buildings which Zococa had noticed from high in the hayloft earlier. 'And that is the San Pueblo Bank.'

Zococa opened the gate and ushered the mounts into the corral next to the barn. Then he noticed Tahoka staring down at him from the loft

50

doorway and smiled. The bandit placed the silver dollars on top of a barrel just inside the large building and then climbed back up the ladder, discarded the poncho and shook the hay from his hair.

'One of those big buildings is the bank, Tahoka,' Zococa said as he pulled his jacket on and strapped on his gun belt again.

The Indian was worried.

They had enough money in their saddle-bags to last them weeks but he he knew that Zococa was now interested in the bank. It made Tahoka nervous as he watched his friend looping the coiled bullwhip over the grip of his pistol.

He began to speak with his fingers and hands frantically but Zococa was not paying any attention. He kept looking at the slanted roof of the barn above their heads. Finally the young bandit found what he had been seeking. He reached up and opened the roof window. Sunshine flooded into the loft as Zococa pulled himself up and disappeared.

Tahoka walked up to the roof window and poked his head out of it. He looked around until he saw Zococa standing on the very edge of the red tiles. The gigantic warrior climbed out from the safety of the loft on to the roof and crawled towards his partner.

He made some gestures with his fingers and Zococa nodded.

'Very true, little one. We are very high in the air

but do not be afraid. I have a plan.'

Tahoka gasped silently as he watched Zococa jump off the edge of the roof and disappear from sight. The Indian crawled reluctantly to the spot where he had watched his friend jumping and cautiously looked over the edge.

Zococa was crouching on the roof of the adjacent building with a broad grin on his face.

'Come on, you old woman. All the houses are practically touching. We cannot fall off but we can get to the bank before those gringos.'

Tahoka pointed to his chest and once again made the shape of a star on his buckskin.

'*Sí*, Tahoka. You are correct. They are indeed Texas law officers. But we have led many of their sort around by the noses in the past, have we not?'

Tahoka frowned as he followed the bandit to the next building and they both stepped across on to its roof.

'I understand what you are saying, Tahoka. We are very fortunate that these men are not chasing us but seek another named Weaver. But is this not a perfect time for us to show them that the great Zococa and his trusty *amigo*, Tahoka, are two of old Mexico's best bank robbers?'

The Apache held on to his friend's wrist tightly until their eyes met. The grim eyes of Tahoka burned like torches into Zococa's face.

'Well, we could be, if we had ever bothered to try.' Zococa shrugged.

SEVEN

John Harrison Weaver had not wasted a single minute since he had led his team of men into San Pueblo. It was now Saturday and the bank would remain closed until Monday morning. This was the duration of the time that he and his men had to execute their daring enterprise.

Weaver knew that a new day must have already started yet the light did not penetrate where he and his crew had made their operational base.

Forty feet below the festive streets of San Pueblo the seven men had set up their base deep beneath the surface of the sun-baked city. They had already started their work following Weaver's detailed instructions.

Already they had broken through the bedrock foundations of the city far above them and inched their way closer and closer to their ultimate goal.

Using the knowledge that they had gained in Tamaulipas, Weaver and his men knew that they would reach the vault of the large bank within twelve hours. They had worked out to the nearest few inches where they would break through the foundations and enter unseen into the place where Mexico kept so much of its wealth.

It had been only eighteen hours earlier that John Weaver had ridden straight through the city with his six inconspicuous followers. They had made their way to the fast-flowing river that lay two miles south.

Once reaching the banks of the deep river the riders quickly located the massive sewage outlet and led their mounts and equipment up into its heart. They had the plans of the entire sewer network to guide them and these, cross-referenced with the maps of the bank high above, told them a where and when to start their tunnelling.

Weaver knew that unlike in many other cities, the mayor of San Pueblo had built his sewers to only serve the richer part of the city. There were probably less than a score of buildings linked to the underground channels. Therefore it was quite simple for him and his men to reach the exact spot that they had pin-pointed on their master plan.

The water from a stream far above them had been diverted into the red-brick tunnels and flowed continuously along the floor of the system never more than three inches in depth.

John Weaver had noted the chimneys that were built into the roof of the red-brick tunnels leading to the surface, allowing all the dangerous underground gases to escape harmlessly. This was the work of men who had known their business, he thought.

Men such as those who surrounded Weaver; men who were skilled in many things but mostly they knew how to take orders from the genius that had led them from the mediocre salaries they had been paid back in Delaware, to the richer harvests of the banks in Texas.

Men such as Tad Smith, an expert with explosives. Don Ford, a man who assisted Smith. Billy Hart, the man who could cut his way through any metal object ever built. Sam Goodwyn had discovered acids and how they could be exploited to burn through anything in order to reach their goal. The remaining pair were probably the most important: Vinny Bell and Kyle Ranson were demolishers. They would take anything apart that Weaver told them to. They all knew that they were equally important and none had ever exchanged a cross word.

John Weaver had made camp on a ledge above the continuously flowing water that moved through the huge sewer system. Their horses were tethered in the water but actually seemed to like the water lapping over their hoofs after so many miles of riding through the scorching desert.

They had brought everything they required with them except the one thing they had arranged to have delivered in less than twenty-four hours.

It had already been arranged that the paddle-steamer would tie up close to the mouth of the sewer outflow. John Weaver and his men would load their horses, equipment and newly found riches on to the boat.

Then they would make their casual escape before anyone was any the wiser. It all sounded so simple, but it required perfect timing on the part of every single member of Weaver's small group of people. The men who were with him in the red-brick tunnels could be relied upon to keep their part of the unwritten bargain and complete their designated tasks on time.

Weaver was hopeful that the captain of the river-boat would be as punctual.

With an eighth share of whatever the men managed to take from the San Pueblo bank vaults, Weaver had little doubt that the paddle-steamer would turn up exactly when arranged.

Everything had been planned down to the small-est detail.

But Weaver had not added McQuaid into his equation.

EIGHT

Zococa slid helplessly down the red-tiled roof. He could feel his spurs scraping on the baked clay roof as he desperately tried to halt his progress towards the edge and its sheer drop. He hovered for several seconds on the very edge of the roof before managing to kneel down. His heart pounded beneath his shirt. He stared down at the twenty-foot distance between himself and the sun-baked cobbles. Zococa glanced over his shoulder at the cautious face of Tahoka, who was peering over the arch of the roof behind him.

The young bandit held up his hand to the terrified Indian. 'Stay there, little one. This is not the place for someone such as you. Someone who is built to walk on the ground.'

Tahoka did not require telling. There was no way he was going to try to emulate Zococa. The massive Apache was staying exactly where he was.

Even for one with such a daring nature, this was not exactly where Zococa wished to be. He had assumed that all the buildings in the street were built so close together that they were practically touching.

From the roof of the barn it had looked that way.

Zococa had thought that he could simply run over each of the roofs in turn until he reached the the bank itself. It had almost proved a fatal mistake.

Then he saw the posse below him as they reached the front of the bank. His curious nature wished he was close enough to overhear their conversation as they inspected the sand-coloured building.

Who was this Weaver and his gang whom the marshal had mentioned to his men? Zococa had heard of most of the outlaws who roamed both sides of the border, but the name of John Weaver meant nothing to him.

Zococa stared at the large edifice opposite him and knew that this was no ordinary bank. It would take more than a few carbines to breach its defences. But it had a series of very tempting flag-poles protruding from above every one of its second-floor windows.

The bandit had no idea why, but he removed the bullwhip from his gun handle and uncoiled it. Holding firmly on to the thick grip, Zococa flicked the whip at one of the flagpoles opposite his precarious perch. With the length of his arm added to the long braided leather weapon, the

whip covered the distance between the two buildings easily.

Its sharp tip was like the tongue of a sidewinder
as it wrapped around one of bank's poles firmly,
allowing Zococa to take the strain.

Zococa gripped the whip with both hands and
leapt from the building's roof and floated through
the morning air until his boots landed on the wide
sand-coloured ledge.

He released the whip from the pole and then
climbed up the face of the building until he
reached the roof of the huge bank. Zococa waved
to the grim-faced Tahoka before heading for the
roof doorway. It was locked but posed little problem for the skilled fingers of the bandit.

Zococa made his way down the stone steps as
quietly as he could until he reached another
locked door. He pressed his ear up against the
wood and listened; there was no sound. With the
long thin skeleton key he kept hidden in the brim
of his sombrero, Zococa picked this lock too.

The bandit opened the door and looked carefully up and down the corridor. He instantly knew
that this must be the private quarters of whoever it
was who ran the bank. The plush red carpet was
over an inch thick and Zococa felt his boot-heels
sinking into its pile.

Zococa did not like it. It reminded him of how
he had felt when he had awoken in the loft of the
barn. His curious eyes stared up and down the
exquisitely decorated corridor. This place was

unlike any he had ever set eyes upon.

With the agility of a puma, Zococa moved up and down the corridor listening at each of its many doors. Then as he pressed his ear to the last one, he heard the voice of a singing female.

Zococa looked up and down the corridor quickly and then tried the golden door-handle. The door was unlocked. As Zococa pushed it ajar he caught the fragrant scent of bath-oils.

Cautiously the bandit entered the large apartments and headed towards the sound of the singing female. He walked silently from one room to another until he saw the enamel bathtub and the long black hair that draped over its end. The bathtub was facing the window and Zococa was able to approach unseen and unheard.

Whoever she was, she was beautiful, he thought. Zococa looked down on her naked body lying in the almost blue water of the expensive tub. He had seen many females in his time but never one with such a perfect body. Licking his lips, Zococa stepped up behind her and knelt down on the damp carpeting. He placed his hands on her shoulders, pushed her upright and started washing her back with a soaped towel.

'Ah, at last you have chosen to return, Juanita,' the female said. She arched her back as Zococa continued rubbing the soap into her soft, perfect skin. 'I thought that you had forgotten all about your mistress.'

Zococa carefully pulled her back until her

shoulders rested against the enamel surface of the tub and then stroked her long black hair, which hung to the floor at his knees. He stared at her lovely body as he stroked her temple gently with his fingertips. Her breasts were small but firm and her waist tapered before her shapely hips. The black tuft of pubic hair was little more than a teasing wisp as it floated in the steaming water.

Zococa continued massaging her brow with the fingers of his right hand as his left hand slipped down her long neck.

'Oh, this is most relaxing, Juanita,' she sighed heavily as the experienced fingers did their magic.

The bandit's hand hovered over her left breast as Zococa wondered if he should tease its erect nipple. Before he had time to make up his mind, the sound of the door behind him caused him to pull back.

'Who is that?' the female asked, opening her eyes and turning her head.

Zococa held her jaw with his fingers and kissed her soft lips quickly before rising to his feet.

'What's going on?' her stunned voice asked.

Zococa smiled down at the girl and then at the maid who was entering with a jug of hot water in her hands.

'Excuse me, *señorita*. I think Juanita has arrived.'

The naked female tried to cover herself as Zococa walked backwards out of the room. He paused by the maid and touched her grinning face.

'Who are you?' the female called out from the bath.

'I am Zococa. Who are you?'

'How impertinent!'

'She is my mistress, Maria Calverez, Zococa.' The maid blushed as she gazed longingly into the handsome face. 'Her father is Don Carlos Calverez, the banker.'

'Beautiful and rich too.' Zococa laughed. 'And with such a pretty maid.'

'Call the guards, Juanita!' Maria Calverez shouted to ears which were deaf to her.

'It is true about the famous bandit,' Juanita said with a coy smile tracing her lips. 'You are as bold and daring as all the stories say you are.'

The bandit nodded as his eyes were torn between looking at the maid and her shouting mistress.

'If this is a bank, where is the safe?'

'That would be in the cellar,' Juanita answered as the long finger of Zococa touched her soft cheek.

'The cellar?' Zococa repeated the word as his finger traced down the maid's neck.

'*Sí, señor*. That is under the building,' Juanita added.

His eyebrow rose. 'I know that.'

'Call the guards, Juanita! Call the guards!' Maria Calverez fumed as a mixture of anger and longing surged through her young veins.

The noise of the guards' heavy boots running

across the marble flooring in the next room alerted the bandit that he had to flee in haste. He bowed to the two females.

'*Adios*, pretty ladies.' Zococa laughed before disappearing around the luxurious drapes and running into the corridor. The athletic young man raced up the steps and then closed the roof door and used his skeleton key to relock it behind him. He knew that this would buy him less than a minute of time to think of how he was going to make his escape.

Zococa rushed across the roof and then noticed a long rope tied between the two buildings. He could hear the heavy boots of the bank guards on the stone steps behind the roof door.

Then the pounding of their rifle butts and shoulders resounded as they tried to force it open.

At least fifty colourful flags hung from the rope. The bandit climbed up on top of the roof wall and looped his whip over it.

Zococa looked down at the street below him. He realized now how much taller the bank was compared to the building where he could see Tahoka waiting for him. The US marshal and his posse were in the street looking up. Even they could hear the furious guards' rantings.

'I think you are in big trouble, Zococa!' he said to himself.

Holding on to both sides of the whip as it rested on top of the rope, Zococa watched in horror as the roof door finally succumbed to the pressure of the bank guards. Rifles were waved around in the air as the half-dozen men stumbled out on to the flat surface.

Luckily for Zococa, the morning sun blinded the men as they emerged from the interior of the bank. Yet this did not stop them from cocking their weapons and seeking out the daring intruder. With bullets raining in all directions, the bandit knew that he had no choice but to leap off the building. He had to risk his neck and put his faith in the strength of the rope.

'I am sorry that I have no time to stop and chat, *amigos*,' the bandit shouted at the men who wanted his head.

Zococa kicked himself away from the top of the bank roof, clinging to his whip. He slid down the rope towards the other building at a tremendous speed.

It was as if rifle barrels suddenly appeared from every one of the windows at the front of the bank's magnificent façade, each of them firing their lethal lead up at the bandit as he grew closer and closer to where he could see Tahoka's startled face peering over the roof summit.

With flags slapping his handsome face, Zococa hurtled at the smaller building.

Then one of the bank guards' bullets got lucky. Zococa saw the bullet sever the rope and felt himself falling through the air. Somehow, Zococa landed feet first on to the red tiles and immediately began climbing up the steep incline. Bullets tore up the roof tiles, showering him with red dust as he reached out and grabbed Tahoka's outstretched arm. The massive Indian pulled the lighter man over the top of the roof and dragged him away from the angry bullets.

'I think they have no sense of humour, *amigo*,' Zococa said, brushing off the the tile-dust that covered him. He coiled up his bullwhip and hung it over the grip of his prized silver pistol.

Carbine bullets shattered the tiles as both men slid to safety.

Tahoka frantically pulled his partner to where the bank guards' bullets could not reach either of them and then used his fingers and hands to ask where Zococa had actually been.

'I was inside the private quarters of the banker, my little one,' Zococa replied honestly. 'I have been bathing a beautiful female. It was most amusing.'

Tahoka shook his head as they walked back across the rooftops towards the barn and then asked if he had stolen anything.

'Just a kiss, *amigo*! Just a kiss!'

NINE

There was something about the army fortress which lay behind the San Pueblo bank that alarmed Lucas McQaid and his men as they entered the main gates. There were reputed to be a thousand men within its solid walls but apart from a handful of men walking around the high battlements, the place appeared alarmingly devoid of life. Unlike most Mexican military strongholds, this place had an air of doom about it.

At first McQuaid tried to shrug off the feelings which had first been voiced by his posse. But he secretly shared their misgivings.

There was no place that the seasoned lawman had ever visited which came close to this one. It felt to the big marshal that he was not taking his men to meet a military equal but actually leading the ten Texans into the jaws of Hell itself.

Lieutenant-General Ramon Garcia had a reputation that had spread even to the middle of the Lone Star State for being a fair and just man who also happened to have more than a thousand soldiers at his command, a famed military leader who had survived more than a dozen bloody battles, before accepting the relatively peaceful post.

After meeting the banker Don Carlos Calverez in the luxury of his private offices, the sight of the fort came as an utter shock to McQuaid. Its impressive walls were on the same scale as that of the bank and their design and finish showed the same skilled hand, but whatever had once been within the large structure was now, for some unknown reason, just a distant memory.

There was a stench within the walls that made the marshal and his deputies nervous. The filth that marked the interior was in total contrast to the sand-coloured walls' exterior.

If a building could actually die, then this one seemed to be in the throes of death.

But why? None of it seemed to make any sense to the eleven Texans as they seated themselves on empty barrels and waited.

Lucas McQuaid had heard of the wealth that San Pueblo enjoyed but there was little evidence of it here inside the courtyard of the fort. The soldiers all looked as if they had not seen a square meal for months and there were far too few of them. Where was the massive force that was meant to protect the prosperous bank?

Marshal McQuaid chewed on the stem of his pipe and silently pondered the fort.

What was going on here?

He had come to San Pueblo to find John Weaver

and inform the banker and the city's military leader that he had the blessing of the highest Mexican court, yet all thoughts of the bank robbers evaporated from his mind as he and his men waited for the duty guard to come take him to meet Lieutenant-General Garcia.

It proved to be a long wait.

For more than an hour the Texas lawmen patiently chewed and smoked their tobacco, voicing their concern to the seemingly emotionless marshal. If McQuaid had learned anything during his years of handling men, it was never to show them that you shared their fears.

He had to remain strong. Solid. Like an anchor. This was the only way to keep ten very different men in check. It was the only way one man could control ten others.

McQuaid knew his job but even he was feeling troubled at the situation he had led his followers into. Without saying a word to his posse, he had flicked the leather safety loops off his matched Remingtons' gun hammers.

If trouble reared its ugly head, he would be ready.

As the marshal's pocket-watch chimed for noon, McQuaid stood and stared at his confused men.

'Somethin' here ain't quite right, boys,' the marshal finally admitted to his deputies whilst he watched the scruffy sentries walking along the parapets. 'I ain't never seen such a motley bunch of so-called soldiers in all my days.'

'Maybe Mexicans don't cotton to washing their uniforms,' one of the posse mumbled.

'It looks that way,' the marshal said.

Ralph Lee sucked on his cigarette and stared around with troubled eyes. He too had experienced many things during his thirty-six years in the saddle, but nothing that had prepared him for this place.

'I don't like this place one bit, Lucas,' Lee said. 'I got me a feeling that we're in trouble.'

The rest of the posse agreed noisily.

'What we doing here anyway?' Charlie Black asked the marshal, who had finished yet another pipe of tobacco. 'What has this dump gotta do with the bank robber John Weaver, Marshal?'

McQuaid tapped his pipe on the grip of one of his Remingtons and rubbed his face.

'I heard tell that there's a tunnel from this fort straight into the bank vault, Charlie,' the marshal replied, blowing down the stem of his pipe before placing it in his deep pants-pockets.

Another of the posse named Gil Lowery stood up from one of the empty black powder barrels that were scattered around the courtyard and cleared his throat.

'A tunnel? You figure that's right?'

Lucas McQuaid raised a bushy eyebrow.

'Sounds doubtful on the surface of it, but when you figure that both this and the bank were designed and built by the same people, it just might be true.'

70

'And if it does exist, Weaver would have wanted to use it to get into the bank vault.'

Lee inhaled the last of his cigarette smoke and then dropped it on to the ground.

'If they are joined up, how come these soldiers ain't borrowed some of that gold and cleaned the fort and themselves up?'

McQuaid smiled.

'Yeah, that's a darn good point. But my main interest is in finding out if Weaver might also have learned about this tunnel and maybe weaselled his way in here. He could be here already, working with these critters to steal a whole lot of money.'

'Maybe that's where all the other soldiers are,' someone suggested, 'under the ground with Weaver digging their way to El Dorado.'

'It's a good theory, but it don't stop this place from being so damn scary.' Gil Lowery sniffed. 'I wanna get out of here, Marshal.'

'If we catch this John Harrison Weaver in the act of busting into that bank, we'll share a $20,000 reward set up by the First National in El Paso.' Lucas McQuaid could almost taste the reward money. It was that close.

Each of the trail-weary faces around the marshal wore the same expression. For the first time, they could see some sense in their mission.

The sound of the door that led to the stone-built officers' quarters opening echoed around the parade ground. The posse all turned and looked with trepidation at the two soldiers who came

71

marching out across the vast littered expanse towards them. They were not dressed like any of the other troopers that the lawmen had so far encountered.

This pair were clean and their uniforms immac-ulate. When they reached the dust-caked deputies and their marshal, the one with the most military ribbons spoke.

'*Señor* McQuaid?' he asked.

The marshal nodded and rested the palms of his hands on the grips of his guns. Now he was even more confused. This pair looked like peacocks in comparison to the handful of enlisted men they had so far observed.

'Yep, sonny, I'm Lucas McQuaid. United States marshal,' he confirmed. 'Lieutenant-General Garcia ready to see me now?'

The uniformed man glanced at his confederate before returning his attention to the lawman.

'*Sí*, Marshal McQuaid. Lieutenant-General Ramon Garcia says he will see you now. If you will follow us?'

'You lead the way and I'll follow, *amigo*.' McQuaid spat on the ground and indicated for his restless men to remain where they were as he followed the two officers towards the imposing building. He could hear the rumbling of their concern as he strode across the yard.

Lucas McQuaid felt his heart pounding as he and his escorts reached the large wooden door.

TEN

It felt to Marshal Lucas McQuaid as if he were willingly entering a burial chamber. He was allowing himself to be buried alive. Upon moving into the dark officers' quarters, the marshal felt his blood chilling as he heard the door being bolted behind him. Now, even if they wanted to, his men could not reach him.

McQuaid glanced over his shoulder and saw the face of the captain staring straight at him. The huge bolts could have secured an ancient castle drawbridge.

The soldier walked past the lawman silently and then moved with his comrade deeper into the dark building. The marshal noticed that none of the wooden window shutters was open. It was dark and the smell of dampness filled his nostrils.

As he trailed the two Mexican soldiers further into the interior of the gloomy edifice, he noticed that only the odd oil-lantern illuminated the place. Their wicks were turned down so far, the small flickering flames barely lit up the narrow corridor.

'How come you folks don't open them shutters?'

McQuaid asked the two officers who were leading him quietly along the dark corridors. 'It's a real bright day out there. Seems a shame not to let some of that light in here. It might take the smell of mould out of the air.'

Neither of the neatly dressed men responded to the words of the law officer. They just walked deeper and deeper into the gloomy interior of the fortress. McQuaid had noticed that the shutters were nailed down even before he had asked his question.

The burly lawman began to feel more and more uneasy with the situation he had willingly walked into. The corridor grew darker as the three men moved further away from the last of the few oil-lanterns.

The eyes of the seasoned lawman had begun to focus as at last they arrived at a large wooden door. McQuaid knew that they must be in the very centre of the massive fortress building. The first soldier knocked on the door three times, then paused for a few seconds before knocking once more.

McQuaid recognized a signal when it was so obvious. The thing that troubled him, though, was why one was required. What was behind the peeling painted wooden surface?

There was a pause from inside the room beyond the door that felt like an eternity to the Texan.

The door was opened from within. A thin tall soldier in dress uniform ushered the three men into the dark room. This room was no brighter than the corridors that had led them here, McQuaid thought.

The marshal felt a cold shiver tracing up and down his spine as he studied his surroundings. He had been into many forts on both sides of the Rio Grande before but never one like this.

He assumed that this must be the officers' mess, yet few details were obvious in the dim light.

In the centre of the room a large rectangular table dominated and had place settings for twenty-two people. Bone-china plates and silver cutlery were laid out expertly on a fine linen cloth.

Three large candlesticks were placed at equal intervals in the centre of the table but none of the tall candles was lit. As the marshal followed the silent pair of Mexican officers slowly passed the hardback chairs, he noticed that all the candlewicks were white.

None of them had ever been touched by a match.

Was this some macabre nightmare?

McQuaid seemed angry with himself for not being able to work out what was going on. He was a man who thrived on puzzles but this seemed beyond even his ability to fathom. He racked his brain trying to understand the clues which he knew were all there before him.

Yet none of it made any sense.

A single oil-filled lamp gave the only light and stood at the very end of the long room on a dusty dresser. A tray with many crystal glasses stood next to a decanter filled with a red liquid.

This entire fortress was full of contradictions. Squalor and luxury standing shoulder to shoulder.

It was loco.

One of the soldiers pulled out a chair when McQuaid reached the end of the table near the lamp and pointed with a white-gloved hand at the wooden seat.

'Please sit here, *señor*.'

McQuaid felt the roof of his mouth going dry as he seated himself on the chair. He removed his Stetson, placed it on top of a plate and then casually looked around him. It was not easy to see anything but he could make out a few features that alarmed him.

There were three tall windows along the south wall but all had heavy black drapes covering them. As if to ensure that not one speck of daylight managed to penetrate the room, the drapes had been nailed to the wooden window-frames from top to bottom. The marshal tried to moisten his lips with his tongue but nothing seemed to help. Only fear of the unknown could dry a man's mouth like this, the lawman mused.

McQuaid felt the hairs on the nape of his neck tingling as the two men who had escorted him here stood behind him. He vainly concentrated his attention at the soldier near the closed door but the shadows hid all except his uniform's brass buttons from the marshal's prying eyes.

Then came some knocks on the door. It was

exactly the same signal that one of his escorts had used to gain entry. Three knocks and a pause followed by a final single knock.

The lawman felt sweat running down his back beneath his dusty shirt.

Lucas McQuaid squinted through the darkness and saw the white-gloved hands of the thin soldier open the door.

At first it appeared as if a most impressive uniform had swept into the room mystically, but on closer inspection the Texas lawman's eyes managed to see the faint outline of a man's face and head as the figure sat down.

They were at opposite ends of the table.

'I am Ramon Garcia, Marshal McQuaid,' a voice said.

A thousand questions raced through the mind of the lawman as he looked down the length of the table at the figure obscured by the three candlsticks and the eerie darkness.

'Thanks for seeing me, sir.'

The officer leaned forward in his chair and rested his jaw on top of his knuckles.

'What is it you want of us?' Garcia asked.

The lawman cleared his throat. 'Didn't you read the letters of authority that I gave your captain, General?'

'I did. They are nothing more than official scraps of paper stating that both our governments know why you are here.' The man leaned back in his chair and accepted a glass of wine from the thin soldier. 'I repeat my question, what do you want?'

'I've heard a rumour that there is a tunnel leading from the cellar in the bank to the one beneath your fortress,' McQuaid said, trying to watch the man's reactions. A man who was simply too far away to focus upon.

Garcia laughed and rested the glass down on top of his plate.

'I too have heard of this rumour, *señor*. That is all it is, a rumour. There is no truth in it.'

Marshal McQuaid felt uneasy as a glass of the wine was placed at his elbow by the thin soldier who was in charge of the door to this black room.

'You mean that it ain't true? There's no tunnel?'

Ramon Garcia gave a huge sigh.

'There is no tunnel leading from our cellar to the bank, Marshal McQuaid. I keep the wine and supplies down there. I have inspected the entire area a hundred times since first arriving in San Pueblo. It is just a myth. Nothing more.'

The lawman sipped at the wine in the crystal wine-glass. It was unexpectedly good and must have cost a lot more than their budget would have allowed for, he thought.

'May I see the cellar, General?'

'I am afraid not.'

There was something in the tone of the voice which made the lawman sit back and not press the soldier. He had heard many stories of this man's military genius and of how he always led his men from the front. This was not a man to rile.

Garcia stood and bowed.

'Our business is concluded, Marshal McQuaid.'

Before the Texan could reply, the senior officer strode across the room and was allowed out by the thin soldier. The man closed the door after Garcia had gone.

McQuaid finished his wine and stood up. The soldiers readied themselves to escort him through the dark mysterious fortress once more.

There were still a thousand questions burning into his craw.

ELEVEN

Zococa had not touched any of the meal before him. He chewed on the end of his long thin cigar. The handsome bandit was deep in thought and knew that he could not rest until he had once again set eyes on Maria Calverez. Whatever the risk.

But how?

It was impossible.

Zococa had watched Tahoka finishing his meal and wiping his mouth along the back of his sleeve. He indicated his own untouched plate. The Indian accepted his partner's meal as it was pushed across the table towards him.

'We must try and gain entry to the bank, *amigo.*' The bandit's words stunned the Apache, who stopped chewing and glared at him in disbelief.

Tahoka dropped his knife on top of the cold steak, and spoke with his fingers.

'The bank is very big, I agree. It is also very well-guarded as you point out so noisily. The money is in the safe which is in the cellar, which is underneath the building. Everything makes even trying to rob the bank totally suicidal but I think that we can get in.'

The Indian warrior picked up the wine-bottle and took a long series of swallows before he continued signalling his objections to the young bandit.

Zococa nodded as he watched his friend's hands' frantic movements. Then he placed his own hand on Tahoka's.

'You are giving me the headache, little one. I understand that we do not have to rob the bank but it is not just the gold and silver coins that tease me. I have seen the beautiful female who lives on the top floor of the building.'

Tahoka waved a finger at Zococa.

'I am not wishing to risk our lives just to make love to her, Tahoka, but if that were to happen, I would not resist. It would be cruel of the great Zococa to deny her the pleasures that only I can give a woman. No, *amigo*! I have seen the riches that are in those private quarters. We do not have to break into the safe, there is a fortune in lovely objects just littering the place.'

The Indian made a few gestures.

'Do not mention the strong lady in the cantina. I wish to forget what happened last night. If I had not been so tired, I would have been able to fight her off.'

The hint of a smile traced his rugged face as Tahoka lifted the knife from his plate and began sawing the steak into large chunks. He was not angry but he was very concerned. How many times had they risked their lives simply because Zococa had seen a pretty face?

The Apache had lost count.

'Of course we could not steal the bank furniture, that is too big and heavy,' Zococa said to himself. He struck a match and cupped its flame to the end of his cigar. He sucked in the smoke and then looked around the small cantina. 'I know what you are thinking, my little rhinoceros. You think that we could probably find the banker's wallet up there in the big apartments. I can read your mind.'

The Apache rolled his eyes and continued eating.

'Of course, you are right. To get back into the building using my trusty whip is out of the question. I do not think it could take your weight. Then there is the problem of finding a ladder long enough to reach the top floor of the bank. I know this is the way that you would do it, but I must insist we think of another way. You are so daring, it troubles me sometimes.'

Tahoka chewed and swallowed a piece of his steak and then angrily tore a loaf of bread into two chunks before mopping up the gravy on his plate. His eyes were fixed on the bandit who was brooding through the smoke.

'Why do you make the faces? Am I not trying to work this out so that we will not get ourselves killed?'

Tahoka interrupted. The young bandit read his friend's silent words and then nodded.

'You are right. They did shoot at us with their rifles. I had forgotten about that little episode.' Zococa flicked the ash off the end of his cigar and stared around the cantina. This one had just one cook. A man with a white beard. He gestured to the old man for more wine.

Zococa accepted the bottle from the man and smiled. 'How many guards are there in the bank, *señor?*'

The elderly cook seemed startled. It was a question that he actually knew the answer to, but had never once been asked in all the years he had been in the large city.

'I think there are at least forty guards, *amigo.* There might be more. They work in shifts.'

Zococa shrugged. 'What are shifts, my ancient one?'

'There are always guards there. Every eight hours they change the guards,' the cook informed the interested bandit.

'How do you know this?' Zococa enquired curiously.

'They all come in here when they have finished their shift before going home to their ugly wives.'

'The poor devils.' Zococa sighed.

Tahoka shook his head when he saw his partner's eyes brighten.

Zococa tossed a few coins to the cook and touched his brow in salute. The old man walked

84

back into the cooking area of the cantina and continued the work which never ceased.

'So the guards come here, my little one. You know what this means? It means that we can get them drunk and find out all the secrets of the bank.'

The huge Apache pushed his plate away and then helped himself to one of his friend's cigars. He rammed it between his teeth and then struck a match with his thumbnail. He sucked in, blew a long line of the strong grey smoke at the ceiling and then banged his fist on to the table.

Zococa raised his eyebrows at Tahoka's display of frustration.

'It was your idea.' He laughed.

TWELVE

John Weaver held the detailed plans in his outstretched arms and looked at them with the keen eye of one who once was the most respected man in his field.

The dim light of the lantern flickered behind him as the rest of his experienced team gathered around him. They had been working without stop for the better part of a day and it showed.

Every man was now tired and yet there was no rest for them until the boat arrived. This was the way they worked; the way that it had to be. There would be plenty of time to rest when the job was completed.

Billy Hart rubbed the grime from his face and then leaned on Don Ford's shoulder.

'We managed to break through the last of the bedrock ten minutes back, John,' Hart explained.

Weaver glanced at the metal cutter.

'Have you reached the metal walls of the vault yet, Billy?'

'We came up across a thick cement-and-metal rod cage,' Hart said, sighing heavily.

Weaver moved his plans closer to the lantern. 'A cage? There ain't no reinforced cement cage on this plan.'

The other men watched as Weaver waded through the pile of other plans that they had carefully copied back in the records office at Tamaulipas.

'Nope. None of these has a cage on them,' Weaver snapped.

'It's there though.' Hart nodded.

'How thick?'

Tad Smith licked his dry lips. 'I drilled through it. It's a yard thick.'

Weaver turned to his men. 'How long will it delay us cutting a hole through it?'

Smith shook his head.

'It'll take too long, John. I suggest you let me and Don blow a hole in it.'

John Weaver hated changing his plans but knew that there was no choice if they were going to complete their task on time and have the gold ready when the paddle-steamer arrived.

'Tad's right. We ain't got enough time to cut through that stuff. We'll have to blow out a hole in the cage and then we can get to work on the vault itself.'

Vinny Bell and Kyle Ranson ambled passed the men. They were heading out to the fresh air with their saddlebags over their shoulders.

'Where are you boys going?' Weaver asked loudly.

'We're gonna cook up some ham and beans, John,' Vinny Bell replied as they waded through the running water. 'Our work starts when Tad blows a big enough hole to get me and Kyle into the vault.'

Weaver nodded.

'Good idea. Tad and Don don't need us around while they're rigging their charges. We'll all wait outside.'

Tad Smith rubbed his hands together. At last he was going to be able to do what he did best. He was going to show how an expert with explosives could blast a hole in the side of a reinforced cage without anyone above them hearing.

John Weaver walked down the large sewer pipe towards the last throes of daylight. Another day was coming to an end and they were behind schedule.

Whether they were ready or not, Saturday night was approaching fast. He had to ensure that they did not waste a single minute of what time was left.

THIRTEEN

The cloudless heavens seemed to be aflame. The sun began to set over San Pueblo as once again the streets came to life with the crowds who were headed for the evening's bullfights in the massive arena.

There was a blissful ignorance in the faces of the people, who were totally unaware of what was happening in their city. Music drifted out over the prairie from the very heart of the city as tens of thousands of people filled San Pueblo's streets. They rejoiced at yet another evening of festivals celebrating the ancient ritual.

The sky was crimson above the two riders as they headed away from the large city in search of anything that might tell them where the bank robber John Weaver and his followers were holed up.

Zococa and Tahoka drove their horses in a wide circle around the city.

They had plenty of time to kill before the guards from the bank would visit the small cantina for their evening ritual.

The young bandit held on to the reins of his powerful pinto stallion and allowed the animal its head. His companion's black gelding trailed a few yards behind the tail of the black and white horse.

Yet even after almost encircling the boundaries of the city, they had found nothing.

Where were the men whom the posse had been searching for all the way from Texas?

It had still been daylight when the pair of bandits had left the San Pueblo barn. Now the two horsemen watched the torches being lit all over the colourful city to their right. Night came swiftly to the barren wastelands that surrounded the prosperous Mexican metropolis.

They had ridden for more than two hours when Zococa decided that their mounts needed a drink and a rest. The bandit pulled gently back on his reins and the faithful steed stopped in its tracks. Tahoka eased his own horse up at the side of his young friend.

Zococa glanced at the hands of the Indian and nodded.

'If this John Weaver and his men are camped away from the city, we should be seeing their camp-fire when the sun disappears, little one.' Zococa threw his leg over the neck of the eighteen-hand-high horse and slid to the sandy ground.

The two men watered the horses and waited for the cloak of total darkness to envelope the prairie.

There was nothing to see.

'Where could they be, Tahoka?' Zococa asked

his friend as his eyes searched the darkening horizon for any sign of the men who had drawn the Texas lawmen like flies to a garbage heap.

There was not a single flicker of a spark from a camp-fire to be seen from where the two riders had stopped.

'This is most strange,' Zococa announced as he stepped into his stirrups and mounted the stallion once more. 'They have to be out here somewhere because otherwise they would be in San Pueblo.'

Tahoka gathered his reins then gripped his saddle horn and hauled himself up on to the gelding. He gestured to his friend who watched the Apache's hands carefully in the starlight.

'*Sí*, little one. We asked at least a hundred people if they had seen a gang of gringos and knew where they were staying. These men are not in the city, but they were.'

Tahoka kicked his heels into the sides of his mount and started the animal moving on. Zococa trailed the mute brave on the tall pinto.

They knew that many of the city's citizens had witnessed the bank robbers riding through San Pueblo but not one had seen any of them stopping.

Even to Zococa, this meant that Weaver had continued on to a secret destination.

But where was that secret place?

Zococa knew it had to be outside the bustling city. A gang of gringos could not hide in San

93

Pueblo during the bullfighting season. It was impossible.

The two riders turned their horses and headed towards the high sandy rise that had prevented the large city from being flooded since the first sod had been laid.

Zococa dragged his horse to an abrupt halt as he saw Tahoka raising his right arm. The Apache was looking over his shoulder at him as the gelding slowed to a stop. Tahoka still retained the keen skills he had honed over the years.

The younger man allowed the stallion to draw level.

'What is wrong, little one?'

Tahoka sniffed at the air and stood in his stirrups, trying to see in the blue light of a million stars. His head turned around as he sought their prey and finally he pointed down at the riverbank about two hundred yards away. Even in the half-light, the flames of the fire could be seen and the aroma of ham somehow managed to obscure the acrid scent of the sewer outlet.

Zococa rested his hand on the shoulder of his friend.

'Excellent, *amigo.* You have managed to find the men we have been seeking. I think we have found out where our *Señor* Weaver and his gang have been hiding.'

The huge Indian reached out, grabbed his friend's right hand and used his own fingers to tap out his questions on the palm of the bandit's hand.

Zococa listened to the silent words that he felt on his skin.

'Why are they here, you ask? I think that these men are digging their way beneath the great bank, *amigo*. Look at the camp-fire lighting up their stinking tunnel. These bank robbers are just like the gringo marshal said. They are very enterprising but not as clever as the great Zococa.'

Tahoka used his hands again to ask what his smiling partner meant.

'They will do all the hard work for us,' the pinto rider explained. 'When they are finished and gone, I think we will find a lot of golden coins waiting for us to simply pick up.'

Tahoka grunted. This was a plan that he actually liked.

The younger rider turned his reins and aimed the head of his horse in the direction of San Pueblo. Zococa waved for his friend to follow.

'Come on, *amigo*. We have work to do. Weaver and his gang are not going anywhere for a little while and we still have a few bank guards to ply with wine.'

The two horses thundered back across the sand towards San Pueblo.

FOURTEEN

Zococa froze to the spot. Few had ever managed to get the drop on the famous bandit before, but that counted for nothing in the scheme of this unexpected turn of events. Zococa felt the cold steel barrel of the Remington gun barrel against the back of his skull just after he had dismounted from the tall stallion.

The interior of the barn was dark and the unsuspecting two bandits had not imagined that Marshal McQuaid and his ten deputies would be lying in wait for them.

'Git them hands up, Zococa!' the marshal ordered as he noticed his men coming out of the shadows with their guns trained on the tall Apache and the still smiling Mexican.

Zococa raised his hands and felt his pistol and whip being removed from his left hip.

'But why would you think that I am the great Zococa, *amigo*?' he lied. He turned his head and peered at the lawman from beneath the large black brim of his sombrero. 'My name is Luis

Santiago Rodrigo Vallencio.'

This statement was met with the sound of gun hammers being cocked. The sound echoed around the barn, making both Tahoka and Zococa feel very nervous.

McQuaid pulled out a crumpled wanted poster from his pants pocket and shook it until it unfolded.

'Says here that Zococa is left handed,' the marshal looked down at the hand-tooled holster on the bandits left hip, 'and rides with a very big Apache Indian.'

Zococa looked at Tahoka.

'Where did he come from? Who are you, big Indian?' he asked the Apache warrior. He turned to the lawman again. 'I have never seen this Indian before, *amigo*. I think he must have followed me. Why do you not let him go, Marshal?'

McQuaid stepped into the torchlight that cascaded into the barn from the busy streets. To the bandit's surprise, he was smiling.

'I ain't after you, Zococa. You ain't worth enough.'

The handsome bandit's face looked insulted.

'Not worth enough?' he repeated. 'That must be a very old wanted poster. I am worth . . .'

'I thought that you said that you weren't this Zococa character?' Lucas McQuaid screwed up the poster and threw it to the ground. 'I got me bigger fish to catch, sonny. Men who are worth big bucks to me and my men.'

Zococa was confused.

'How did you know that I was here? What do you want of me if it is not the reward money on my head?'

'I seen you flying through the air from the bank this morning. Mighty impressive,' McQuaid said, trying not to laugh.

'And you thought that only the great Zococa would do anything so daring?' Zococa asked.

'Or dumb,' Charlie Black chipped in from behind the massive Tahoka.

'I asked a few folks in the bank and they told me that Zococa had somehow managed to get inside the private quarters of Don Carlos's daughter.' The marshal emptied the bullets from the silver pistol and then handed it back to the surprised bandit along with the coiled whip.

'What do you want with the great Zococa?' the Mexican asked. He looped the whip over his holster, into which he slid the silver pistol.

'I just don't want you boys interfering and spoiling our chance of making some real money,' the marshal said.

'Is that all?' Zococa felt a rush of relief flowing over him and his heart started beating steadily again.

McQuaid stepped closer to the bandit and pushed the Remington into Zococa's guts.

'I could kill you here and now, if'n I had a mind,' the marshal said.

The bandit nodded.

'This is true. What else do you want of Zococa?'

'You are as smart as all them stories I've heard about you, sonny. I want some information and I figure that you can provide me with that information.'

Zococa nodded again.

'If I can provide you and your well-armed men with the knowledge you seek, I will.'

'Where is Weaver?'

'You think that I know this?'

McQuaid pushed the gun barrel harder into the stomach of the still-smiling outlaw. It hurt and the pain showed.

'I don't wanna waste bullets on you, sonny. Just tell me where them bank robbers are and I'll forget that I ever set eyes on you or the redskin.' The lawman was no longer showing any signs of amusement.

'We bandits have a code, *señor*. We do not tell tales on our fellow thieves,' Zococa said through gritted teeth. He stared hard into the older eyes before him.

Lucas McQuaid returned the gaze and whispered, 'I'll give you five twenty-dollar silver coins if you tell me if you and your friend know where Weaver is. That's a hundred dollars sonny.'

'*Sí*. That is exactly a hundred dollars, *amigo*.'

'Well?'

Zococa tilted his head and lowered his hands.

'Money does make a little difference, Marshal. Now I am not just informing on fellow villains but doing the business. I always enjoy business. Those you seek are camped down by the river's edge. They are making the tunnel to the foundations of the bank.'

McQuaid pulled his arm back and holstered the Remington. He pulled the five silver coins from his vest pocket and dropped them in the palm of Zococa's left hand.

'Much obliged.'

'Business is business.'

The eleven lawmen left the barn and then led their mounts from the corral. They silently mounted and spurred their horses away from the building. Soon they disappeared into the crowd of people who were heading towards the bullfights.

Tahoka moved to the side of the smiling bandit and looked at the smaller man with concern. The huge hands of the Apache pulled the bandit into the light from the street as he searched for injuries.

'Stop fussing. I am fine, my little rhinoceros,' Zococa said. He bit down hard on to the silver coins, one by one. They were real and they would soon pay for all the wine he intended to pour down the throats of the bank guards.

He had learned long ago that nothing loosened tongues like free wine. Zococa intended to find out as much about the bank as he could.

FIFTEEN

Maria Calverez's eyes widened in disbelief as she looked out from one of the windows of her luxurious apartment. The sight of the two men heading towards the bank against the sea of people that were making their way to the bull-ring, stunned her.

'Are you ready, Maria?' Don Carlos Calverez called from the corridor.

Maria did not reply to her father. She had opened her mouth but no words came out. The sight below her had taken her breath away.

Zococa was returning.

Was he insane? She tried to call out but the recollected taste of his lips reminded her that this was no ordinary bandit who was approaching the bank. This man dared to do whatever he wanted for the sheer hell of it.

Even though he was dressed in the uniform of one of the bank guards, she recognized the bandit. The giant beside Zococa looked equally out of place in his ill-fitting uniform but she had eyes for only one of the bold bandits.

Don Carlos Calverez entered his daughter's rooms and walked across the highly polished marble floor towards her. Juanita tried vainly to get the attention of her mistress.

'Have you gone deaf? I asked you if you were ready.' The banker checked his golden pocket-watch. 'I think we will make it before the bullfights start but we have to hurry. The coach is in the courtyard.'

Maria looked briefly away from the window and forced a smile at him. She was like so many other daughters. She could do no harm in the eyes of a doting father.

'I am sorry, Father. I thought I saw someone in the street whom I had met before.'

Calverez seemed infuriated for a brief moment.

'When do you meet anyone without my knowledge, Maria?'

She turned back to the window and stared down into the street but Zococa and his companion were gone. Maria pressed her face to the glass and attempted to look straight down. It was impossible.

'He's gone,' she blurted out.

'Who's gone?' Calverez pushed passed her, opened the window and leaned over the ledge and glared down. The crowds were still filling the streets. 'Whom did you see?'

Maria accepted her black lace shawl from her maid and started for the open doorway.

'Come on, Father. We do not want to miss the first fight. I might be presented with the ears of the bull.'

Reluctantly the banker closed the window and followed his beautiful offspring.

'Who did you see, Maria?' he repeated.

'I made a mistake,' she lied. 'I did not see anyone. It was just a trick of the light.'

Juanita watched her two employers leaving, then rushed across the lavish apartment. She knew that only one man could have caused her mistress to lie to her doting father.

As she headed into the servants' stairwell, descending as quickly as her legs could carry her, Juanita knew that Zococa had returned.

This time she wanted him all to herself.

It had taken four gallons of wine but Zococa had managed to drag every scrap of information he required from the drunken bank guards inside the cantina.

With one of the twenty-dollar coins, the bandit had managed to bribe the old cook into stacking the drunken guards in the dark alley behind the cantina.

It would take many hours before any of them would be sober enough to notice.

Zococa and Tahoka had stripped the garments from two of the larger guards and used the bright blue-and-white uniforms to disguise their own clothing from the eyes of those they might encounter if they succeeded in getting inside the bank. Exactly what Zococa thought he could or would do even if he did get inside, was a mystery even to himself. There were so many questions that the bandit wanted answered.

Would the men whom the Texan marshal was hunting actually be able to break into the bank vault?

Was it John Weaver and his gang down by the river, or just a bunch of drifters?

The bandit led his silent companion through the shadows and into the bank's dark courtyard. He pulled the key-ring off his belt and studied the keys. They were all big enough to fit into the large lock, he thought.

Zococa felt the massive hand on his shoulder.

He turned and stared at the face of the Apache. It was troubled. Tahoka looked ill at ease in the uniform which did not fit any part of his gigantic body.

'Try to look smaller, *amigo*.'

The humour did not sit well with the warrior but before Tahoka could respond, he spotted the approaching vehicle over the head of Zococa. The Apache pointed at the elegant coach that was coming from the bank's stables and just entering the secluded courtyard.

Tahoka dragged the bandit into the protection of the dark shadows.

Zococa gritted his teeth and stared at the coach. It was fit for a queen and had probably cost a king's ransom. When the matched pair of white horses were brought to a stop outside the elegant glass-panelled door, both outlaws could see that it was decorated in gold leaf.

'That is a very pretty coach, Tahoka,' Zococa said in a hushed tone. He watched a guard opening the door and then ushering the two people towards the vehicle.

The young bandit went to move away from their hiding-place but was restrained by the massive hands of the Apache brave. They both stared at the banker, who was dressed in black, then their attention fell on his daughter.

Even Tahoka was taken back by her stunning beauty. The huge mute Indian looked at her and felt sadness overwhelming him. It seemed like a lifetime since he had been able to satisfy any woman but there were still haunting memories.

Memories that tortured his mind almost as much as the knives of his enemies had tortured his body.

Tahoka sighed heavily and remembered how he had been saved by the bandit beside him. Yet he had had more than his ability to speak taken from him that day, by the swine who had ruthlessly tortured him.

Whatever it is that makes a man a man, Tahoka no longer possessed. Like his tongue, that too had been savagely cut from his body.

'Is she not splendid, *amigo*?' Zococa asked as the coach was driven past their hiding-place in the dark archway.

Tahoka nodded.

Zococa pushed one key after another into the lock before finding the correct one. He turned it and heard the tumbler release the bolt.

Before opening the door, the bandit looked into the eyes of his comrade. Even in the darkness, Zococa could see that his friend was still troubled.

'You can go back to the barn if you wish, little one. You do not have to risk your own life for my madness.' Zococa smiled.

Tahoka remained at his friend's side and pointed stubbornly at the door.

'Let us see if it is possible to get close to the fortune that lies within these walls, *amigo*.' Zococa winked and pushed the door open. They entered silently and began to move around the cold corridors where no paint had been wasted on walls that only servants and guards would see.

Zococa thought of the stark contrast between this and the lavish luxury he had witnessed up in the private suites of the banker and his daughter. He paused.

'I have just thought of something. Even if we do manage to steal the gold from this bank, the gringo marshal will blame the man named Weaver. Is this not amusing?'

Tahoka nodded.

They continued on cautiously. The younger man led his partner down a dimly lit corridor and wondered what lay behind the door which faced them at its end. It was cold but sweat dripped from the brows of both men.

'This place is very eerie, is it not?' Zococa said in a low voice, though Tahoka was close enough to hear. 'I am beginning to think that we might be much smarter if we returned to the old barn.'

Tahoka pointed at the door and grunted. He was curious as to what lay behind it.

'You wish us to continue, little one?' Zococa raised both his eyebrows. This was the first time that his friend had ever shown any daring in all the days that they had been together.

Tahoka nodded his head slowly up and down and pointed at the door-handle.

'Very well, I shall open it and we shall see what lies beyond.' Zococa reluctantly placed his hand on the handle and silently turned it.

The door opened towards them and Zococa eased himself through the gap to take a look. He had expected to see guards but there was still no evidence of them.

Then the sound of running feet coming down stone steps greeted his ears. He squinted into the shadows.

Zococa drew his pistol and cocked its hammer.

The footsteps grew louder. The large Apache pointed to their right. Both men could just make out the bottom of a crude stone staircase.

'You are right, Tahoka. Someone is coming down from one of the upper floors.'

The Indian touched his own ear and then made

109

a few hand movements. He could tell that it was a female on the stairs by the sound her small feet made.

'A girl? I hope you are right. I would hate for it to be a man with tiny feet.' Zococa screwed his eyes up and tried to focus.

Suddenly Juanita reached the ground floor and headed towards them. She ran through the half-light straight into the arms of the smiling bandit. Zococa grabbed her and placed his hand over her mouth.

To his surprise she did not try to scream.

His perfect teeth smiled down on her. 'You?'

'Zococa!' Juanita gushed when he slipped his hand off her mouth. 'It is I, Juanita.'

'Juanita. Such a pretty name. It suits you.' Zococa felt her body melt into his own. He lifted her up until their lips met.

'You are indeed as your legend says you are.' She sighed heavily as he released his grip.

'You were expecting us?' Zococa suddenly realized that their presence was no shock to the pretty maid. If she knew they were here, then possibly others did.

Was this a trap?

'*Sí*, Zococa. My mistress spotted you from her apartment before she left for the bullfights with her father,' Juanita explained. 'But she did not betray you. Your lips ensured that.'

Even knowing that Maria Calverez had said nothing to her father about seeing him heading back towards the bank, Zococa still felt uneasy.

The bandit began to question himself.

Why was he here at all? Was it for the kisses of the female he had watched leaving in the coach? Was it because he knew of the bank's reputation for being impossible to rob? Did he want to prove that Zococa could do what no one else had ever managed to do and break into the San Pueblo bank?

Every sinew in his body was warning him to get out of here while he still could.

But Zococa did not heed his own misgivings. For the excitement of the adventure was still driving him on towards a fate he knew would one day claim him.

'Where are all the guards who are meant to protect this place, Juanita?' Zococa heard himself ask the maid.

She stroked his cheek and tried to kiss him again. 'There are two who guard the private quarters of Don Carlos and the rest remain guarding the doors that lead down to the bank vaults.'

Zococa felt curious. They had come this far and were so close to the fortune that lay below their feet. It was said to be impossible to breach this bank's defences, but it was so very tempting to try.

Too tempting for the Mexican bandit.

'Can you take us to one of those well-protected doors, my pretty one?' Zococa asked as his lips brushed her brow and tasted her soft skin.

'But if you try to break into the vault you will

surely be killed,' Juanita said. Her bosom rose and fell at an ever increasing pace. 'There are three well-armed men on each of the two secured doors which lead down to the cellar, Zococa.'

He bent his knees slightly, cupped her buttocks in his hands, then stood upright again. He buried his face in her cleavage and kissed her soft breasts in turn. If he was going to die, he wanted to do so with the flavour of a beautiful female on his lips. Juanita pulled his face up and devoured it with her eager lips.

'I cannot let them kill you, Zococa,' she said. Her bosoms heaved as he stroked them with his face.

'They will not, my pretty one,' Zococa reassured her as he felt her kisses moisten his face.

'But how can you be so sure?' Juanita gasped.

'Many have tried to kill me, Juanita. It is not as easy as it would seem.' He slowly lowered her to the floor. 'I am like the cat with nine lives.'

'How many lives have you left?'

He grinned broadly. 'That I do not know.'

She glanced at the massive Indian who stood in the shadows watching them and listening out for any trouble that might head in their direction. She was curious.

'Before I take you where you wish to go, please tell me something, Zococa,' she said.

'Anything, my pretty Juanita.'

'Who is this big quiet Indian?'

Zococa smiled at Tahoka and then looked into

her glistening eyes. Her perfume was still in his nostrils.

'This is Tahoka. He is my very best friend.'

SIXTEEN

Deep within the bowels of the army fortress the truth was far more terrifying than any of the rumours that had circulated in and around San Pueblo over the past six months. This was a place of horror; humanity had been sacrificed to something far more cruel.

If civilized men had been able to reach this unholy place, they would have not believed the sight which greeted their unsuspecting eyes. Those who had once been soldiers of the emperor were now slaves in chains. Those who still survived were stained by their own blood as whips lashed their already scarred bodies whenever they tried to rest for even a few seconds.

The dead were piled up in corners waiting to be carried to the surface and thrown into yet another hastily dug mass grave. Even Satan himself could not have devised a more evil place.

But this place had nothing to do with the depths of Hell. This was the work of depraved men, not the Devil. Men who had somehow managed to step over the boundaries of sanity in their mad quest for gold.

Lucas McQuaid and his deputies had pondered the same questions as had troubled so many of the city's citizens. Where were the thousand men who had been stationed inside the fort? Why did the garrison building have all its shutters closed, even during daylight?

Why did Lietenant-General Ramon Garcia act in such a strange way?

The answer to all of these questions and many more were buried deep beneath the fortress itself. For this was where the greed of a score of officers had spilled like poison over the innocent enlisted soldiers and the unsuspecting fortress commander himself.

Like something out of a medieval horror story, the men who now controlled the fort and its military budget had managed to take the life of the real Garcia and his most loyal officers. They had struck like the messengers of pure evil. Quickly and without regret.

Mercilessly they had killed the famed Ramon Garcia whilst he slept, over six months earlier. Their reason was simple: he had begun to suspect what twenty of his officers were planning.

Yet Garcia had made the error of branding his rogue officers with his own morality. He had given them the benefit of the doubt.

It had been a fatal mistake. His first and last.

The twenty mutinous officers had acted swiftly

to quell all who were not of their own persuasion. The bodies of more than five hundred of their enlisted men were buried in shallow graves a few feet beneath the sand of the parade ground, each one in turn killed by a razor-sharp blade to the throat. One by one the officers had disposed of their opponents.

The acrid aroma of decaying bodies still haunted the huge parade grounds. Death had its own scent, one that refused to weaken as the days grew steadily into weeks and then months. Nothing could stop the stench of rotting flesh.

McQuaid and his deputies had recognized the smell within the fort but their minds, like so many others in San Pueblo, had also refused to acknowledge the truth.

No sane mind could.

If they had, they might have questioned what had happened to a once peaceful military outpost.

Why had the officers risked everything in order to take over this particular fortress? That was simple. They had discovered that the stories of the tunnel which linked the bank and the fort together, were actually true.

It had been designed and built as an escape route for the banker and the vast government stockpiles of gold and silver. An insurance policy which would have allowed a thousand troopers to enter the bank vaults and forestall any would-be robbers.

But shortly before the two buildings had been

completed, a nervous bank official had ordered the tunnel to be blocked up. His reasoning was simple: if soldiers could storm the bank through the secret tunnel to protect the fortune that lay in its vault, they could also do the same to steal it.

All official records of the tunnel had been erased from the plans of the two structures. Thus, it only existed in the memories of those who had worked upon it. The stories of the tunnel had become regarded as merely tall tales.

It had remained that way for years until two of Garcia's officers, working in the huge cellar, had discovered the end of the blocked-up tunnel against a wall.

No amount of white paint could hide the truth from their eager eyes.

Soon all of the officers knew of the discovery and it was not long before fate moved its great hand. Greed has always been one of man's most bitter companions. Most can keep it from ruling their lives but others fall under its spell and soon destroy everything in their path, just to satisfy its ravenous appetite.

They had the scent of the bank's massive vaults in their nostrils and knew that they had to try and get to the gold which was only one hundred yards away.

But when a hundred-yard tunnel has been blocked by hundreds of tons of rubble, it becomes more like a hundred miles.

This was why the cellar beneath the massive

garrison building had been turned into the most pitiful place on earth. What remained of the fort's enlisted men were now little more than slaves. They were beaten and forced to continue their relentless digging into the tunnel until they dropped.

Now scarcely more than a hundred of these men survived in shackles. They were lucky to get any food whatsoever as their cruel taskmasters whipped them as if they were animals.

Yet few would have treated animals with so little respect. The score of officers had managed to take over the fortress by killing all who stood in their way. They had managed to make their slave labour dig until they were only a dozen or so yards from the foundations of the bank.

The vermin who had met Marshal Lucas McQuaid ought to have known that a man of his intelligence would not be as easily fooled as most.

Yet he had gone away, as had everyone else who had managed to gain entry into the fort since they had killed Garcia. They knew that their time was running short.

Soon officials from the government would come to San Pueblo to inspect their properties.

The vicious whips of the officers had to beat their victims into working even harder than they had ever been called upon to do before. They had to reach the bank's swollen vault and then they could use their arsenal of explosives to blast their way to riches.

It had seemed so simple six months earlier when they had slit the throat of Ramon Garcia.

SEVENTEEN

Lucas McQuaid drew his reins to his chest and stared down into the darkness below them. They were there all right, exactly as Zococa had claimed. The camp-fire still smouldered and now the seven horses were tied up behind tall brush. John Harrison Weaver and his crew must have already reached the place that they had sought, McQuaid thought to himself as he sucked on the stem of his empty pipe.

They had to be inside the red-brick tunnel.

The starlight danced across the fast-flowing river as the horsemen gathered around the marshal. He weighed up the situation.

He knew that it was no hastily dug tunnel that he and his posse were looking at, but the outlet to the city's crude sewer-system.

His nose told him that.

Even from a few hundred feet's distance the unpleasant odour was making his horse nervous.

Now McQuaid had a problem. If Weaver and his men were inside the belly of the sewage system, how could he get them out? Or should he not even try? Perhaps it made more sense to allow them to finish what they had started and simply arrest them when they emerged with their loot?

At least that would then prove that Weaver was the man who had more than likely robbed the Texas banks. McQuaid knew it was not positive proof but it would be more than enough for any judge north of the Rio Grande to order John Weaver and his men's necks to be stretched.

Even now the Texas lawman wondered if he had worked out the puzzle correctly. Would it be the elusive Weaver whom he would find down there?

Few clues had been left behind them in Texas. Only the evidence that each of those robberies had been done by men who were skilled engineers.

It had to be Weaver!

The brooding marshal got down from his saddle and held the nose of his nervous horse until each of his deputies had also dismounted. None of their horses cared for the smell of this place. It was like that of a dozen outhouses when the quicklime had run out.

'What's the plan, Marshal?' an anxious Charlie Black asked whilst checking his guns.

'We take it nice and easy,' McQuaid replied, soothing his skittish mount. 'I don't wanna spook them *hombres*. We have to let them achieve their goal, boys. If we go in too soon, they'll just stop and we won't be able to prove a damn thing.'

'But they could take hours,' Ralph Lee

protested. The deputy was sore and tired and had
wanted to rest his bones before doing anything.
'I'm tuckered out.'

A few of the other posse members mumbled
their agreement with Black's words.

'Then get your bedrolls off the backs of your
horses and get some shut-eye. I'll wake you if
anything happens.'

Gil Lowery stared hard at the marshal. 'We
thought that we'd be spending tonight in a hotel,
Lucas.'

'That's what you promised,' Lee said as he
untied his bedroll from behind the saddle cantle.
'You said that we'd have a big feed, a bath and a
sleep in a soft feather bed before we had to do
anything.'

'Them bank robbers ain't been resting up none.
They're busy and could be coming out of that
stinking hole any damn minute with their arms full
of Mexican gold.' McQuaid pulled out his tocacco
pouch and started filling the corn-cob bowl. 'I
don't reckon they'll wait for us to pamper
ourselves.'

Ralph Lee tossed his bedroll down on the
ground and then pulled his Winchester from its
scabbard.

'We need someone down there to keep an eye
on them critters, Marshal,' he said.

'You volunteering, Ralph?' McQuaid asked the
deputy.

'Yep.' Lee began his slow walk down the sandy

slope towards the remnants of the distant camp-fire.

McQuaid placed his pipe between his teeth.

'Anybody got a bottle of whiskey they wanna share?'

EIGHTEEN

Reluctantly, Juanita led the two bandits along the cold corridor towards the west wing of the bank. She raised her finger to her lips and then paused at the last corner between the trio of well-armed guards and herself.

Zococa placed his hands on her shoulders and eased her back until she was between Tahoka and himself.

The handsome bandit straightened the baggy uniform that covered his own clothes. Carefully he pushed his face to the wall junction and stared with one eye at the three men who were standing before the well-constructed door.

It was nearly thirty feet to the smoking bank guards. Too far for anyone to run and successfully overwhelm another without being shot first. It was also too far for him to walk towards them in his borrowed uniform without their realizing that he did not belong inside the bank.

Zococa leaned back and stared at his two companions.

'I do not think that I can reach them.'

Juanita placed a hand on his chest. 'But I can, Zococa.'

His eyebrow rose and he smiled. 'I think you could, but this is not right. Tahoka and I shall leave.'

Tahoka nodded in agreement.

She did not listen but stepped around the bandit and pulled at the sides of her dress and undergarments until they were as wide as she could make them.

'I think you can get very close to them, if you hide behind my petticoats, Zococa.'

Juanita then loosened the drawstring on her white bodice until her well-proportioned breasts were released.

The eyes of the bandit fell from the attractive face of the maid down to her moist heaving chest.

'What are you doing, my pretty one?'

'This will distract them long enough for you to act.' She smiled.

Zococa nodded feverishly.

'I think this will certainly distract them.'

She walked to the corner and Zococa crouched down behind her flowing skirt.

'Are you ready, Zococa?' she asked quietly, staring under her left arm at the handsome face behind her.

The bandit did not reply with words. His fingers pinched her rear and she started walking with a sudden jolt. A rush of excitement welled up inside her. She had never done anything as bold as this before.

Tahoka waited at the corner and listened for his cue to come charging at the guards when Zococa managed to strike.

The three guards had not expected this night's eight-hour shift to be any different from all the others which had preceded it, but the sight of the gorgeous Juanita made them change their minds.

To weary eyes, this was not just a woman, this was a vision. They dropped their cigars and stepped on them as they drooled over her. The three guards all licked their lips as they watched her approach them. This was Juanita the maid as none of them had ever expected to see her before.

Their eyes fixed on the shapely breasts as they bounced in and out of the white bodice. She was teasing not just their sight but every other part of the guards' senses.

'What are you doing here, Juanita?' one of the smiling men asked as she drew closer to them.

'I have come to see which of you are real men.' Her smile made their chests swell up inside their blue-and-white tunics.

'But we are all real men,' another of the guards cooed as his eyes devoured her body.

'You wish to prove it?' Juanita had never realized the power she had over the opposite sex until this moment. Now she was actually enjoying the attention the three drooling men were paying her.

It was only when Juanita felt the hands of

Zococa pushing her forward towards the eager guards, that she actually remembered why she was here at all. This was not just a game that she had willingly entered into, this was something far more serious. If it went wrong, people would certainly die. She stared at the guns in the holsters on their hips and felt desperately out of her depth.

'I . . .I think it is very late,' she mumbled as fear stroked her.

'Come here, Juanita. I give you something to remember,' the oldest of the men boasted. 'Something very, very big.'

Suddenly Juanita felt frightened. The men before her wanted more than she would ever give them. They did not wait for her to come to them, they moved towards her quickly.

As their hands grabbed out at her, she heard the voice of Zococa over her shoulder. Then his silver pistol jabbed out at the closest guard face.

The sound of the gun hammer being cocked took the smiles off the three faces.

'Greetings. That is enough, *amigos*. Now you will lie down on the floor and place your hands behind your backs,' the bandit ordered.

'Who are you?' one of the men asked.

'Do you not recognize the great Zococa?' The bandit smiled.

Juanita covered herself up and went to move away. Before she had time to do so, a guard grabbed at her. The pretty maid felt herself being used as a battering-ram as she was thrust into the bandit.

Zococa went flying across the narrow corridor and bounced off the unpainted wall. Before his body hit the ground, he managed to strike out at the guard's head with the barrel of his gun. The man reeled backwards.

The two remaining guards were going for their guns.

Zococa knew that he dare not fire his weapon without alerting every other bank guard in the massive building that something was very, very wrong. He also knew that he could not allow the two furious guards to do so either.

Pushing the stunned Juanita aside, Zococa started to rise up from the floor when he spotted Tahoka out of the corner of his eye. The Apache warrior was charging down the corridor at the two guards.

Both men suddenly realized that Zococa was not the only bandit in their midst. To be in the path of Tahoka in full flight was like being a matador facing the biggest bull in creation.

The two men were confused.

For that split second of indecision they paid dearly. The Apache threw himself into the two men. His muscular arms were at head height and caught the pair of astonished guards around their faces.

The sound of breaking noses and bones echoed off the walls as the men crashed on to the hard floor beneath the Indian. To make sure that he had done his job properly, Tahoka lifted both men's heads up by their hair and banged them down heavily.

Zococa gritted his teeth as the sound made him shudder.

'I think they are asleep, my little rhinoceros.'

Tahoka got back to his feet and helped the lovely Juanita up from the cold floor. She was dazed.

'Are we still OK?' Zococa asked the large warrior.

Tahoka knelt down and pressed his ear to the cold surface of the cement flooring. He then looked up and nodded before moving back to the side of his partner.

'What was he doing, Zococa?' Juanita asked the bandit.

'He was listening for the other guards. They could not have heard anything or Tahoka would hear their footsteps approaching.'

Juanita leaned against the wall and stared down at the three bleeding men at their feet. Each was dreaming of less painful things.

Zococa knelt and studied the lock carefully.

'You need a key to open that door, Zococa. Only Don Carlos has a key and he keeps it on his person at all times,' the lovely female told him.

Zococa tore off the blue-and-white uniform and cast it aside, revealing his own jacket and its neat collar. His fingers toyed with the edge of the collar until a long fine piece of wire appeared in his hands.

'What is that?' she asked.

'The way of opening that which cannot be opened, pretty one.'

Juanita watched in awe as Zococa slipped the wire into the lock and manoeuvred it around until the lock released.

'How did you do that?'

'The lock has not been made that can stop Zococa.' He smiled, rising to his full height. Gently he opened the door.

Tahoka stared over both their heads into the darkness. He held on to their shoulders and pushed past them. Zococa and Juanita watched as the Indian walked down the steps that led to the bank vault.

'You had better go back to the safety of your mistress's rooms, Juanita,' Zococa said.

'But I want to see what is below,' she insisted.

'This I cannot allow.' The bandit looked down into her dark eyes. 'You have already done too much. When the guards awake they will tell the banker of your presence here. You must say that the great Zococa forced you to bring him here at gunpoint. Otherwise you will be in trouble.'

'I do not mind as long as I am with you.'

Zococa knew that he had no time to argue. He had to make her leave them now or she could end up in real danger.

'Go and wait in your room. I shall come to you when this is over.'

She lowered her head. 'I shall never see you again, shall I?'

Zococa put his finger under her chin and lifted her head until their eyes burned into one another's.

'You will see me again, Juanita. We have yet to make love.'

She turned and ran back along the route that they had used to reach this point. Zococa moved down the steps until he caught up with his silent friend.

'Goodbye, Juanita. I am sorry that I had to lie to you,' he whispered under his breath as she disappeared around the corner.

Tahoka waved his arms at the great expanse before them. A dozen oil-lanterns burned continuously, making the air dry, but neither man noticed.

They could only see the huge bank vault.

'Zococa is not going to ruin his reputation by trying to pick that lock, *amigo*.' The bandit sighed, throwing away the wire lock pick. 'It takes a man to recognize his own limitations.'

The two bandits made their way down to the floor of the cellar and stared at the incredible metal vault. They had never seen anything quite so serious before. Whoever had constructed this monster of a safe had been deadly serious.

Suddenly the pair heard a noise coming from their right: the sound of picks axing at rubble.

Tahoka grabbed his friend's arm.

'I hear it, little one,' Zococa said, following the Apache warrior to the safety of the corner of the bank vault. Both bandits rested their backs against the cold steel and held their breath.

'Someone is digging their way through the wall, *amigo*,' Zococa said as he glanced around the metal corner of the vault and focused on the tiled wall.

Tiles splintered and then fell from the wall as men forced their way into the foundations of the bank from the tunnel. The rogue soldiers had finally managed to achieve their goal but the cost in human life had been horrendous.

Zococa's eyes narrowed as he looked in disbelief on the bodies' of the half-dead men who had achieved their masters desires. Blood ran from the bleeding lash-marks on their emaciated torsos as the officers started to walk over the bodies of their slave labour.

'Dear Lord,' the stunned bandit gasped.

Tahoka moved to the shoulder of his friend and glared at the unbelievable sight. He knew all about torture and recognized it in all its forms.

Zococa gripped his pistol in one hand and his whip in the other. He walked side by side with his companion towards the officers who continued to emerge from the newly opened tunnel.

'They like to play with the whips, my little one. So does Zococa!'

NINETEEN

The first of the mutinous army officers who had walked over the backs of the exhausted blood-soaked soldiers into the bank cellar, was also their self-proclaimed leader. Captain Jose Verone had discarded Ramon Garcia's uniform when his fellow conspirators screamed out that they had reached the bank.

For six months Verone had played the part of the famed Lietenant-General so well that he had almost begun to believe that he was Garcia.

'Bring the gunpowder, *amigos*!' he yelled down the tunnel to his men. 'We will blow this bank vault apart and be gone before dawn with all of its gold.'

'I think not!' Zococa said as he and Tahoka squared up to the handful of army officers who had joined Verone in the bank.

Jose Verone's head turned quickly. He stared at the two men who faced them. His hand clutched at the long bloody whip as he stepped closer to the bandits.

'Who are you? Are you guards?'

Zococa's eyes trailed over the beaten and battered wretches whom this man and his confederates had mercilessly used to reach this place. It was a sight that turned the young bandit's stomach.

'I am Zococa!'

Crippled soldiers raised their heads and looked up at the handsome bandit. They all knew of the name and suddenly felt that there was hope that they might be saved from almost certain death.

'Zococa!' The name seemed to be exhaled from every one of the prostrate men who lay at the feet of their so-called superiors.

Jose Verone lashed out at the men who chanted the bandit's name but no amount of lashes with his deadly whip could stop them calling out.

'Silence, you animals! Silence!' Verone demanded.

Soon the other officers began whipping their victims with equal ferocity. They too screamed at the bleeding men to stop chanting the name of the famed bandit but they too failed.

Zococa and Tahoka held their guns firmly in their hands.

'I shall surely kill you if you continue hurting these men.'

Verone stared hard-eyed at the bandit. He had spent six months giving orders, not taking them. He was damned if he was going to listen to a man with a price on his head.

The bandit raised his pistol.

'I mean it, *señor.*'

For a moment it appeared that Verone had heeded the warning and he gestured to his fellow officers to stop whipping the half-dead victims at their feet.

'The great Zococa is very big when he holds a pistol on his enemies. I wonder how big you would be if you did not have that pistol?'

Zococa tilted his head and smiled.

'But I do have the pistol, *señor.* And when I say that I will kill you, this is not a threat, but it is a prophecy.'

Verone exhaled heavily and turned sideways on to the pair of bandits. For a split second he looked dejected.

Then faster than either Tahoka or Zococa could even blink, the man cracked his long whip in one swooping movement and ripped the guns from both their hands.

Suddenly the chanting stopped and Verone's laughter started. 'Now we are going to see how big a man the great Zococa really is,' he roared.

Zococa glanced at the blood flowing from the back of his left hand. He then passed his own whip from his right hand into his left and allowed it to uncoil at his feet. He gripped hard on to the thick end of the woven leather weapon.

Tahoka was about to move forward to Verone when Zococa cleared his throat and made the Indian look at him.

Zococa watched his friend's eyes staring at his right hand as he moved his fingers quickly. He had signed a secret message to the giant Apache.

A message that the warrior understood and would obey.

The officers all began to walk closer to their chosen leader. Soon they surrounded Jose Verone. Each man held on to their own whips. Each man glared at the pair of bandits.

Zococa spoke with his fingers again and Tahoka moved backwards away from his partner and the wall of ruthless killers.

'Look, *amigos*.' Verone laughed loudly. 'The Indian is now not so brave.'

Zococa lifted his bleeding hand to his mouth and sucked the blood away from the brutal cut. He then lowered his arm and gripped on to the whip.

'You might be correct, *señor*.' Zococa forced a smile. 'You know how Indians are. They are so fickle.'

Verone raised his arm and swung the whip over his head before lashing out at the bandit again. The sound of it cracking echoed around the huge bank cellar.

Zococa did not move a muscle, even when he felt the blistering pain of the whip's tongue. Blood began to trickle down his cheek from the inch-long gash above his left eye.

'Now it is my turn,' he announced.

Jose Verone pointed his whip at the bandit angrily.

'You do not get a turn. Let us whip this creature to death, *amigos.*'

Every one of the depraved officers began to loosen their whips again as they trained their attention on the motionless Zococa. He dropped his own whip on to the floor.

'Zococa does not look so great any longer,' Verone joked.

'Now, Tahoka!' Zococa screamed out loudly before dropping down to the floor and rolling toward his silver pistol.

The Apache warrior swiftly pulled his long Bowie knife from his belt. Using every ounce of his strength, Tahoka threw the deadly knife with an anger only he could truly understand or feel.

The blade sped into the shoulder of Verone. He flew backward knocking half his men over before he crashed into the wall next to the tunnel opening.

Before the other army officers could lash out with their whips, Zococa fanned his gun hammer. He hit two of the men dead centre and then rolled over again to get a clear shot at the rest of them.

Verone still had enough willpower left to crack his whip at Zococa again. The bandit ducked as he saw the long tip of the braided leather snapping at his face. This time it was only his black hair that was struck.

When he looked up, Jose Verone had disappeared into the tunnel and was heading back to the fortress.

139

Three of the officers tossed their whips away and drew their guns.

Lead blasted down at the rolling bandit. But each time he rolled, he fired. By the time his pistol was empty, he had killed them all.

Tahoka rushed up to his partner, hauled him off the ground, then picked up his own gun.

Zococa emptied his spent shells from his silver Colt and reloaded quickly.

'We must chase that evil man, little one,' Zococa said, suddenly becoming aware of the soldiers all around them. Once again they were chanting his name aloud. Zococa paused. 'Is it not nice to have so many admirers?'

Tahoka looked at the men who were repeating the name of the young bandit. He nodded at them knowingly.

'Why did these men do this to you, *amigo?*' Zococa asked the bleeding man closest to him.

The man wearily explained. 'They are crazy, Zococa. They killed Ramon Garcia and tortured and killed most of us, just to dig out this tunnel so that they could get to the gold in the bank.'

The bandit glanced at Tahoka.

'I do not like those who torture others, my little rhinoceros.'

Before Tahoka could use his hands to reply, the entire room shook violently. Then the muffled sound of a series of explosions rocked the very foundations of the building. Plaster fell from the ceiling of the bank vault as a massive hole appeared in the wall behind them. Dust and debris hit the two bandits and knocked them off their feet.

TWENTY

Even though the entire bank vault was filled with thick choking dust from the explosion, John Harrison Weaver and his six followers still made their way over the debris into the bank. They were well used to working in such conditions.

They made their way through the choking dynamite residue with a steely determination that only confidence in one's own ability could foster. The seven highly skilled engineers clambered over the rubble towards the massive steel-coloured bank vault, carrying their equipment with them. Tad Smith had done his usual expert job and blown a hole in the reinforced cement cage which surrounded the entire cellar, with very little additional damage.

Now it was down to Sam Goodwyn to use his array of acids to cut through the steel vault as quickly as possible. Each man had their own expertise and John Weaver had little else on his mind when he made his way through the cloud of dust.

The last thing any of the unarmed bank robbers expected was to find other men inside the massive cellar of the bank.

Zococa and Tahoka crawled from beneath the inch-thick layer of cement-dust which covered not only them but the injured soldiers and dead officers. The bandit rubbed his face until he was able to see the new intruders.

John Weaver and his team of men stopped in their tracks and stared at the horrific scene over 200 feet in front of them by the opposite wall. Every man inside the cellar of the San Pueblo bank, whether living or dead, looked like a ghost with the cement dust covering them.

'What's happening, John?' Billy Hart asked Weaver.

Zococa blew the dust from his pistol and stared directly at the stunned leader of the bank robbers.

'You must be the notorious bank robber John Weaver, señor.' Zococa coughed.

Weaver dropped the bag of tools he had been holding and blinked hard. He, like his six-man team, was scared.

'How the hell do you know who I am?' he asked nervously. 'And who are you and what are you all doing here?'

Zococa knew he and his partner had little time to answer questions. Captain Jose Verone was fleeing with every passing heartbeat.

'There is a very big Texas marshal after you and your compatriots, amigo.'

144

Weaver stepped forward. 'How do you know this?'

'I am Zococa, *señor*. The greatest bandit in all of Mexico.' Tahoka cocked the hammer of his gun and pointed at the tunnel eagerly. He knew that Verone and what was left of his mutinous band of army officers were getting away.

As Zococa started into the tunnel, he heard Weaver calling out behind him. He paused and looked over his shoulder at the man who, like his companions, was not wearing any weaponry.

'You say that there's a US marshal dogging our tail?' Tad Smith swallowed hard.

'*Sí, amigo.* He waits outside by the river with ten deputies.' The young bandit smiled. 'I think that if you do blow up that safe, it might be best if you do not return to the river and your horses.'

'But how can we make our escape?' Weaver felt sweat trying to penetrate his dust-caked face.

Zococa looked at the tunnel he was about to enter. 'This way leads to a fort and many, many horses and wagons, *señor* Weaver. But if you do break into the safe, please help my poor friends to safety.'

Weaver looked at the helpless wretches between himself and the bandit. It was a sight that beggared belief.

He nodded.

'You got a deal, Zococa.'

Zococa saluted the man and then ran over the loose rubble that still filled the floor of the tunnel.

He could see that Tahoka was now reaching the end of it ahead of him.

He called out for the Apache to wait but Tahoka was angry and did not intend to slow his progress for anyone. He wanted to get his hands on the brutal men who were ahead of him.

Tahoka was able to straighten up once he reached the cellar of the fortress. He paused for a split second to get his bearings.

Death was all around this place.

In the humidity, even living things rotted.

Its acrid stench turned the huge Apache's stomach. Those who were still alive lay in their own filth and blood, pointing at the steps that led to the surface level of the stone fortress.

Tahoka wanted to help these men but knew he had to find the officers first. There was no safety for any of them whilst those creatures still roamed free above them.

As the Indian placed a foot on the bottom step, Zococa reached the cellar and inhaled the unpleasant odour. The smile fell from his face as he ran to Tahoka's side.

'Come, little elephant. We have unfinished work.'

Both bandits stormed up the steps until they reached a locked and bolted door. The taller Indian looked through the small peep-hole in it and saw the shadows of fleeing men. He slammed his fist into the door.

Zococa cocked the hammer on his silver pistol

and shot the lock apart, but still the door would not budge.

'It is bolted, *amigo!*'

Tahoka pulled Zococa aside and then raised his right leg and kicked it with all his might. The door-frame came away from the wall. Both men pushed until they could get past it and enter the corridor.

Darkness ruled this world. Verone and his men had extinguished all the lanterns as they made their escape.

Like the deafening sound of a thunderbolt, the noise of a gun being fired echoed all around them.

Zococa pushed his large friend to the wall and shielded him with his own body.

'Somebody shoots at Zococa, little one. This they will regret.'

The two bandits returned fire and then continued running after the noisy military boots which they could hear coming from the maze of corridors. Only Tahoka's keen hearing kept them on course.

Another volley of deadly lead traced through the darkness at them, but they carried on.

'We have them worried, *amigo*,' Zococa shouted as he squeezed his trigger again and saw one of the officers reel and fall.

Tahoka and Zococa leapt over the dead officer and ran as fast as their legs would take them until they reached another closed door.

Just as Zococa was about to reach out for the large brass handle, Tahoka grabbed him and dragged him around a corner.

The massive explosion sent burning pieces of wood hurtling past them.

Tahoka used his left hand to tell his friend that his keen nostrils had sensed the burning fuse stuck into the barrel of gunpowder.

'This is not the sort of business that Zococa likes, Tahoka.'

The two men waited for the smoke to clear slightly and then continued on through the narrow doorway. This time they were greeted by a hail of gunfire.

They fell on to their bellies amid the burning wood and started to shoot back.

'How many are there, little one?' Zococa shouted above the deafening noise of the battle.

Tahoka raised five fingers and then caught sight of one of the officers trying to make a break for it. He fired and sent the man hurtling to his doom.

The Apache nodded to himself as another of the men tried to flee from the coridor. He fired twice more and this time his victim was knocked off his feet and went straight through one of the nailed-down wooden window shutters. The body hung on the window-sill.

To the alarm of the military bushwhackers, the light of the parade-ground torches cascaded into the gloomy building.

Zococa could see the remaining officers suddenly rising from their hiding-places now that the light was illuminating them. Without a thought for his own safety, the bandit jumped to his feet and fanned his gun hammer until the pistol was empty. As usual, his aim was deadly.

The two men ran past the five bodies and reloaded their guns. The huge Apache raised his arm and halted Zococa when they reached the corner leading to the darkest corridor. The keen senses of the mute warrior knew that something was wrong and he was not going to allow his friend to run blindly into the jaws of their enemies.

Zococa rested his back against the cold wall and stared into the eerie blackness before them. The bandit knew that they had to be close to the huge parade ground which surrounded the large fortress.

'What do you hear?' Zococa whispered clutching on to his pistol.

The Apache indicated that the remaining officers were down there hidden within the shadows.

Zococa knew that he had only a few bullets remaining on his gun belt apart from the six he had in the chamber of his gun. He could not risk wasting bullets. Neither of the brave duo knew how many of their foes were still alive and waiting to destroy them.

Every shot had to count.

Tahoka fired once into the unknown.

A volley of bullets blasted back at them from out of the darkness. Zococa knelt down and then saw the starlight trailing into the corridor for a few seconds. Tahoka signalled that two of the officers

149

had fled the building by the large door.

'That must be the leader and one of his right-hand men, my little rhinoceros,' Zococa said as another hail of bullets came blasting at them. 'The rats are leaving the sinking ship.'

Tahoka tore the ill-fitting uniform from his chest and rolled it up. He tied the sleeves in a knot, then nudged his friend and nodded.

'What, *amigo?*' Zococa was puzzled.

The Apache reached out and extracted the silver cigar-case from the young bandit's inside jacket pocket. His large fingers opened the lid and withdrew a few of the long matches that Zococa kept there so they would always remain dry.

The sharp eyesight of the warrior had already spotted an oil-lantern a few yards ahead of them. Defying the officers' furious firepower, Tahoka ran and plucked the lantern off the wall and then returned to the cover of the corner.

Zococa watched as his friend wrenched the glass chimney off the top of the lantern and poured the kerosene over the rolled-up garments at their feet. Then he stuffed the glass bowl inside the clothes.

Tahoka struck a match and ignited the bundle. The oil burned furiously. With even more bullets raining down on them, the Apache picked up the weighted flaming uniform and threw it to the very end of the dark corridor.

When the bundle hit the end wall, the glass bowl shattered inside the burning rags. Flaming scraps of clothing and razor-sharp glass rained over the hidden officers, setting their own uniforms alight.

Now Zococa and Tahoka had targets.

Both men fanned their gun hammers. Before the bodies had hit the floor, the two bandits had raced to the huge door and kicked it open.

Zococa pointed to the centre of the parade ground where waited the horses and wagons that had been readied by the three officers who had been doing sentry duty on the high parapets.

The two bandits threw themselves on to the ground and rolled behind one of the many water-troughs as the five remaining men opened up on them with handguns and rifles.

Within seconds the trough was full of holes and water began pouring out over the dry ground.

Tahoka fired until his gun was empty and then shook the spent shells from its smoking chamber. Before he could do anything to stop his partner, he saw the younger man rise to his feet and run towards one of the wagons.

Bullets tore up the ground. Zococa felt one of his spurs being shot from his right boot as he dived beneath the flat bed of the wagon. Spinning around until he was facing his enemies, Zococa gritted his perfect teeth and fanned his gun hammer twice.

He saw one of the men dressed in a frayed trooper's uniform fall lifelessly to the ground.

Zococa was angry with himself.

He had wasted a bullet. Two bullets for only one man. The bandit opened the hot chamber of the silver Colt and pulled out the two spent shells with his fingernails, then searched his gun belt for his remaining bullets. He found two, and slotted them into the pistol and snapped the gun shut. Crawling across the ground beneath the belly of the wagon, Zococa's fingers searched for the last bullet. He found it and slipped it into his vest pocket.

Tahoka had started shooting again from over the top of the trough and was drawing the fire of the four remaining men.

Zococa rose to his feet behind the wagon and then started to run along beside the horses. Before reaching the head of the last horse, the bandit dropped to the ground and fired between their legs.

The chests of the two closest officers burst open as the bandit's bullets tore into them. As they fell, Verone and his last remaining confederate made a dash for the saddled line of horses. Tahoka jumped over the water-trough and ran across the dark parade ground towards the two men. Defying his immense size, the Apache warrior leapt on to the back of the first horse and wrestled the rider until they both fell to the ground.

Zococa bolted out from the cover of the team of horses and fired at Verone. The skilled horseman dragged his reins around and charged straight at the shooting bandit.

The horse reared up as its rider clung to the slippery cavalry saddle. The hoofs of the animal forced Zococa backwards until he fell to the ground.

Jose Verone drove his horse at the fallen bandit. Zococa rolled to his side and blasted his last bullets up at the horseman.

Verone suddenly released the reins and fell heavily off the skittish mount. The would-be leader of the rebellious army mutiny hit the hard ground but found that his right boot was still caught in the metal stirrup.

Zococa managed to scramble to his feet as the horse thundered past him and galloped the length of the parade ground dragging the helpless captain behind it.

The bandit stooped, picked up his silver pistol and emptied the spent shells from it. He plucked the last bullet from his vest and inserted it into the chamber before holstering it.

The sound of a neck snapping dragged Zococa's attention to his kneeling friend as the huge hands finished off the last of the evil officers. Tahoka dropped the lifeless head on to the ground and then stood up.

The two men looked at one another.

Zococa nodded.

FINALE

Marshal Lucas McQuaid steered his horse toward the unmistakable Tahoka who was astride his black gelding outside a small flower-covered house. For the life of him he could not understand how John Harrison Weaver and his men had managed to elude him and his posse. He had waited for more than three hours by the river, before leading his men into the sewer and then through the expertly cut hole into the cellar of the bank. By then, an entire section of the vault had been removed and the bank robbers had helped themselves.

McQuaid had followed the trail through the dust and into the tunnel to the stinking cellar of the fortress. He had noted the bodies but knew that Weaver had nothing to do with them. This had the mark of someone else.

Every question which had puzzled the marshal had been answered fully but he felt no satisfaction in the knowledge he had gained.

He had been stunned to find Zococa and his

silent friend helping the severely maltreated soldiers in the courtyard. The tracks of the wagons John Weaver had used to take the gold from the fortress had been easy to follow but it was a trail that ended at the river's edge. The clever bank robber had left the empty wagons on the shoreline and disappeared.

The paddle-steamer's whistle had told the marshal that his pursuit was in vain long before he and the posse reached the river.

The lawman drew in his reins and stopped his horse next to the large Indian. McQuaid stared at the pinto stallion with the distinctive black sombrero hanging from its saddle horn, next to Tahoka, and then he looked at the house. 'Is Zococa in there?'

Tahoka nodded.

'Reckon he ain't alone.' McQuaid raised a bushy eyebrow and then pulled his pipe from his vest pocket and placed its stem between his teeth.

Tahoka shook his head.

'Is she pretty?' the lawman asked. He struck a match and lowered the flame into the pipe bowl.

The Apache shrugged.

McQuaid blew out a cloud of smoke and then stared up at the window above a tiled porch. It was open and the sound of a female laughing drifted out into the morning sunshine.

Suddenly, above them, Zococa climbed out of the window and paused on the porch roof as a beautiful female kissed him farewell. The bandit walked down the tiles and then jumped down and landed on his saddle.

'Marshal McQuaid, I thought I heard your voice,' Zococa said as he placed his sombrero on his head and pulled its drawstring tightly under his chin.

'You boys wouldn't happen to know anything about that bank robbery, would you?' the marshal asked.

'It was John Weaver, *señor*. Just as you said.' Zococa smiled broadly. 'A most briliant deduction.'

'How come Weaver didn't return to his horses by the sewer, sonny?' McQuaid chewed on his pipe-stem.

Zococa shrugged.

The marshal leaned across in his saddle. 'It was almost as if somebody tipped him off about the posse. I wonder who might have done that?'

Zococa sighed. 'I feel we might never know the answer to that, Marshal.'

The lawman noticed that the smiling young man no longer had his whip.

'What happened to your whip, sonny?' he asked.

Zococa glanced at Tahoka and then back at the older man. 'I do not need a whip, *señor*. It is a cruel weapon.'

McQuaid cleared his throat. 'Anyway, I thought that I'd tell you something before you boys leave San Pueblo.'

'We are listening, *amigo*.' Zococa smiled as he ran his fingers over his thin moustache.

'I wired the Mexican authorities and they were most grateful that you boys saved the lives of those soldiers in the fort,' McQuaid said. 'It took a lot of guts.'

'It was nothing.' Zococa grinned.

'They said that if you boys weren't bandits, they would have given you both a medal,' the marshal added as smoke floated up from his pipe into the dry morning air.

Zococa patted his swollen saddle-bags.

'I have enough medals, *amigo.*'

McQuaid took the pipe from his mouth and stared at the bags behind the saddle cantle of the pinto stallion.

'What? How could you have any medals?'

'There was a box full of them in the fort, *amigo.* So many pretty medals.' Zococa smiled over his shoulder up at the window where the female was still watching him.

'So you stole them?'

'No, *señor.* I borrowed them. It is business. Strictly business. You understand?' Zococa waved at the female and blew her a kiss.

'What would you want with medals, Zococa?' Lucas McQuaid asked.

'I do not want them, but the lovely ladies think they are so very pretty.' Zococa waved again and the ravishing girl above them stood up. She was naked except for a large medal hanging on a colourful ribbon around her neck.

The marshal felt his jaw dropping as he looked

at the very happy female.

'You give them to your girlfriends?'

Zococa turned his stallion around and grinned even more broadly at the lawman.

'Of course. It would be wrong to offer them money but a medal is something that they can cherish along with the memory of having made love to Zococa.'

'You give them a medal for making love to you?'

'I gave Rosita two, *amigo*!' Zococa laughed, gently tapped his spurs into the flesh of the pinto and started to ride away from the house with Tahoka at his side.

'Why two?' McQuaid called out.

'You must be very, very old, *amigo*, if you have to ask a question like that.' Zococa winked over his shoulder at the confused lawman.

The US marshal watched as the two men rode towards the rising sun. Even in the busy streets of San Pueblo he could still hear Zococa's laughter.

McQuaid knew that Zococa was one puzzle that even he would never be able to solve.